She was swept with a surge of passion

She couldn't stop herself from drawing his face down toward her trembling eager lips.

"Emily...oh, Emily! You're driving me insane!" he murmured feverishly, covering her eyes, ears and neck with burning kisses. Her whole being was on fire for him, the blood in her veins a molten stream of white hot desire....

"No!" Ludo tore his mouth away, wrenching his body from her arms with a savage oath. "Can't you see that it's wrong? You're in my care and under my protection," he ground out through clenched teeth. "We mustn't...we really mustn't—ever again. I know I behaved badly back by the waterfall. I should be shot for what I did to you."

"But I wa... " she ma... it is wro...

"But I do... quietly... slowly a... heavy tread.

WELCOME
TO THE WONDERFUL WORLD
OF *Harlequin Presents*

Interesting, informative and entertaining,
each Harlequin romance portrays an appealing
and original love story. With a varied array
of settings, we may lure you on an African safari,
to a quaint Welsh village, or an exotic Riviera
location—anywhere and everywhere that adventurous
men and women fall in love.

As publishers of Harlequin romances, we're
extremely proud of our books. Since 1949,
Harlequin Enterprises has built its publishing
reputation on the solid base of quality and
originality. Our stories are the most popular
paperback romances sold in North America; every
month, eight new titles are released and sold at
nearly every book-selling store in Canada and the
United States.

A free catalogue listing all available Harlequin romances
can be yours by writing to the

HARLEQUIN READER SERVICE
1440 South Priest Drive, Tempe, AZ 85281
Canadian address: Stratford, Ontario N5A 6W2

We sincerely hope you enjoy reading
this Harlequin Presents.

Yours truly,

THE PUBLISHERS

MARY LYONS

the passionate escape

Harlequin Books

TORONTO • NEW YORK • LONDON
AMSTERDAM • PARIS • SYDNEY • HAMBURG
STOCKHOLM • ATHENS • TOKYO • MILAN

Harlequin Presents first edition September 1983
ISBN 0-373-10625-4

CHAPTER ONE

THE NOISY LAUGHTER and conversation of the other guests filled the hot, humid evening air as Emily stood at the edge of the brightly lit, wide stone terrace, looking out over the tin roofs of the Lambouchere Mine buildings and on down into the dark valley below. The African moon slanted through the leaves of an adjacent tree, highlighting the pale sheen of her ash-blond hair and the shimmering silver threads woven into her deceptively simple white dress.

Emily sighed, shifting uneasily as she tried to ignore the small trickle of sweat winding its way down her backbone. What could have possessed her to come out here to this dreadful country? The moment she had landed yesterday at the airport and had walked out of the air-conditioned aeroplane into a fiercely hot and humid wall of heat, she had known it was a mistake to have come to Ouanda. "The land that God forgot," her great-great-grandfather had called it. He wasn't far wrong, Emily thought, wriggling uncomfortably as she felt the material of her dress sticking to her damp slim body.

Opening her evening bag she removed a handkerchief to dab at the beads of perspiration covering her forehead. It wasn't just that she had arrived in the middle of the hot season—your timing is impeccable, as always, she told herself gloomily—but here she was, thousands of miles from civilization, she didn't know a soul and even those few people she had met were plainly awkward and nervous in her company.

Of course she'd always known about Ouanda. As the primary source of her family's wealth, she could hardly not have done so. Formerly part of French Equatorial Africa, Ouanda sat like a giant blob on the map, sandwiched between what had previously been the Belgian Congo to the South and Chad to the North. As far as she knew, her father had never visited the country, preferring to live in solitary splendour, shut away in his large, gloomy house until the day he died.

As for her? Emily sighed wearily. She'd travelled all right, but always on the same boringly wealthy jet-set circuit. It was only lately that she had come to appreciate the truth of her father's favourite quotation: "The wretchedness of being rich lies in having to live with rich people." Perhaps that was why she had been feeling so apathetic and depressed lately? Before coming out to this country she had supposed that in some way Ouanda would prove to be different. Exactly how "different" she hadn't been able to define, but she had hoped that somehow out here in deepest central Africa, she would find something worthwhile. Something that would give her life some meaning and enable her to break free from the endless round of mindless pleasure seeking.

Her illusions had been rudely shattered on the drive from the airport. So much for Shangri-La she had thought in dismay, viewing with horror the conditions in which the inhabitants lived. The sight of houses which were more like cardboard shacks, running open sewers in the streets and a population who seemed, in the main, to be sick and listless had caused her to exclaim aloud in distress. Although she had been assured that there were many Ouandans in a far worse state than those she had seen, she had found it hard to get to sleep last night, her mind being filled with images of the small children whose stomachs were distended with beriberi, their thin limbs covered with sores.

She might not be able to do anything about living conditions in this country, but she was certainly going to make sure, when she paid her official visit to the mine tomorrow, that the black workers employed by the Lambouchere Company were housed decently—or else! Emily accepted a drink from a passing waiter, who took one look at the grim expression on her lovely face and hurried thankfully away.

In the meantime, she told herself, it was no good regretting the fact that she found herself in this benighted country. She knew, only too well, exactly why she had been more than grateful to accept the sudden invitation of the Ouandan government. It was all her own fault, and she'd just have to grit her teeth, stop feeling sorry for herself and try to make the best of the next five days.

Sighing deeply, her nostrils filled with the grey, pungent smoke of the mosquito-repellant capsules burning on the terrace, Emily turned as Andrew Sinclair approached, accompanied by a small fat man in spectacles.

"Miss Lambouchere. I don't think you have met Pierre Monet, one of our technicians." Emily shook her head and smiled faintly at Andrew. A typical Scot with sandy hair and a broad Scottish burr to his voice, he was obviously trying his best to make her feel welcome. As manager of the Lambouchere Diamond Mine here in Ouanda, he really had little choice, she reminded herself wryly as she turned to greet the man beside him.

"Enchanté mademoiselle...." The Frenchman bowed and raised her hand to his lips. And that's another thing about this damned place, Emily thought, the vague headache she'd had all evening beginning to throb more intensely. She really should have done her homework before leaving England. On her arrival it had been a shock to discover that the everyday language of the country was French, a legacy of its colonial past.

It was some three years since she had lost the argument with her trustees: "You cannot own a French company and not speak the language fluently," had been their unanswerable logic. A lanky, painfully shy and deeply unhappy seventeen year old, she had hated every minute of her enforced attendance at the Swiss finishing school. However, as ordered, she had learned to speak fluent French and German. If she now ruefully admitted the wisdom of her trustee's decision, she remembered that it was only being taught to ski which had helped to alleviate the lonely misery of that year in Switzerland.

Continuing to speak as fluently and charmingly as she could to the French technician, Emily was well aware of the part-curious, part-apprehensive glances cast her way by most of the other guests. The women especially, it was clear, had taken one look at her white silk dress and had immediately known it for the couturier model it was. Their sideways glances at the arrival of this rich, well-dressed and startlingly beautiful woman into their closed world thousands of miles from anywhere, would have disturbed most people. Emily, used all her life to such reactions, merely sighed with weary resignation.

So what else is new, she asked herself unhappily. What did you expect? Why should this place or these people be any different from anything else you have ever known?

With a smile, the Frenchman moved away to talk to a colleague. Taking a deep breath and bracing herself, Emily turned to face the guests, assuming a bland, bored expression and allowing the looks of envy and dislike to slide off her shoulders with a much-practiced shrug of supreme disinterest. Hearing a small cough beside her, Emily looked down to find Andrew Sinclair's wife, Amy, by her side.

"Ah, Miss...er...Lambouchere...."

"Oh, please call me Emily. My surname's such a mouthful!" She smiled at the small, nervous woman.

"Yes...well, I do hope that you will be comfortable in the guest bungalow. It's a bit far away from the mine, but...well, that's maybe a good thing, don't you think?" She looked up anxiously at Emily. "I mean...well, there's less noise. We—we should have had you to stay here, of course, only...." Amy faltered unhappily.

Only the thought of having to put up with the titular head of your husband's firm proved too much for you, Emily silently completed the sentence. Poor Amy. She'd looked simply terrified at the airport yesterday, like a small mouse amidst the welcoming committee. She had taken one look at the tall, elegant English woman and had blanched in dismay.

"I'm sure that I shall be very comfortable," Emily smilingly strove to reassure her. "Your husband is giving me a tour of the mine tomorrow morning, which should be very interesting."

"Yes, well...I hope so...." Amy was clearly at a loss as to what to say to her guest. Her face suddenly brightened as she saw the entrance of a man at the other side of the terrace.

"Oh," she smiled happily. "It's Ludovic. I was hoping he could come, but he said he might have to fly out with the rest of his film crew. I'm sorry." She turned away from Emily. "Do excuse me for a moment...." She hurried off to see to the new arrival.

Emily had turned at her words and looked across the terrace. A very tall man stood with his back to her, talking to Andrew Sinclair. He was dressed in a green shirt and long green trousers tucked into boots; she was only aware of a dark head and a pair of very broad shoulders as he gestured and then turned to survey the company.

My goodness! Emily goggled in amazement. That man...well, he had to be one of the most attractive-looking men she'd ever seen. The description of tall, dark and handsome seemed to fit him like a glove!

"Can I get you a drink?" She turned to see a young, blond giant staring at her with admiration. "Man—are you a sight for sore eyes!" he said in a South African accent.

Emily smiled at the man's enthusiastic response to

her presence and began to feel that maybe the evening wasn't going to be so awful after all.

"My name's Bob," he continued. "Andrew Sinclair tells me that you're over here for the coronation—is that right?"

"Yes," she replied in a light, cool voice. "I can't say I really understand the politics of this place, but isn't it a bit unusual for a president of a republic to make himself a king, especially in this day and age?"

"Too damn right it is!" Bob agreed, laughing. "The man's bonkers, of course. So would we be if we had to live here permanently. I'm off on leave tomorrow, down to the Cape. Man, I can't wait to get out of this hellhole, if you'll pardon the expression!"

"It can't always be like this, surely? I've never been anywhere so hot, and as for the humidity...."

"Actually, it's not too bad up here, not too bad at all. It's paradise in fact, especially if you compare this place with the rest of the country. What I can't stand are those damn rain forests. Let me give you a piece of good advice; whatever you do, keep out of the rain forests—they're the pits!"

"There's absolutely no possibility of my going anywhere near them, I'm pleased to say." Emily smiled at the South African. "But I still don't see why General what's-his-name, has decided to make himself a king?"

"Like I said, the man's mad—absolutely raving. Just between ourselves General Georges Ngaro is as nutty as a fruit cake! He thinks he's Napoleon—straight up—and just like Napoleon, he's going to crown himself in three days' time. What's more, not only is he crowning himself, but he's going to do it covered in diamonds! I'm not kidding," he assured Emily as she shook her head in disbelief. "He's designed a cloak which is absolutely smothered in diamonds."

"It doesn't seem possible...."

"Believe me—that's only half of it. There's his crown—nothing but diamonds again—not to mention the damn big coronation ring your company is giving him. A pretty clever idea, I thought. Should keep the old guy sweet for a bit."

"I didn't know anything about that," she said slowly.

"No reason why you should, I suppose. Believe me, the whole affair's going to be a hell of a laugh, or it would be if he wasn't so dangerous."

"Dangerous?"

"Look, give a man, any man, unlimited power, and it's bound to turn his mind. So, you've got a guy who's not entirely sane, to put it mildly, right? Remember Idi Amin? General Ngaro is out of the same mould; he was even trained by you Brits at Sandhurst, no less!" The South African looked down at his empty glass. "All this talk is giving me a thirst. Can I refill your glass at the same time?"

"Yes, please. Just tonic water."

"You're kidding!"

"No." Emily smiled and shook her head.

"Okay. You're the boss—literally!" he said, laughing. "Stay here. I'll be back in a minute."

Emily stood idly looking out into the night, before turning slowly to glance around the terrace. A moment later she found herself staring into the eyes of a man across the room. It was the stranger who had arrived late. However, he must have changed, because he was now dressed in a white evening shirt, unbuttoned far enough to show his deeply tanned chest, and a pair of dark slacks.

Emily was used to being stared at, but she felt her cheeks flushing under the intensity of his gaze. He really was quite extraordinarily handsome, she thought, feeling slightly bemused as his eyes bored into hers. And so tall! He seemed to stand head and shoulders above anyone else in the room, and at five foot ten inches herself, Emily deeply appreciated tall men.

For goodness sake—this is quite ridiculous, she thought as he continued to regard her intently. She sent him a smouldering glance through her lowered eye-lashes, before turning away to look out across the valley. That ought to bring him over, she thought complacently. It was, after all, a technique that had never failed her yet.

The man continued to look at the woman. At her tall, slim figure and the head of pale, silvery blond hair which fell straight to her shoulders. So pale indeed as to be almost white. A faint smile of amusement touched his lips for a moment before he shrugged slightly and moved into the crowd.

"Tell me," a rich, deep voice said moments later from behind Emily's shoulder. "Do you always look so bored or is it just a trick of the light?"

Emily turned slowly. "What do you think?" she asked coolly. A coolness she was far from feeling as she looked up into the man's eyes. Hard grey mocking eyes, carrying no expression except that of mild disinterest, but which nevertheless made her feel breathless and surprisingly nervous. His black hair was thick and curled slightly at the base of his neck, while his deeply tanned face.... There's no doubt about it, she thought in some confusion, he is quite definitely and without exception, the best looking man I've ever seen.

"Let me see," he said, placing a hand beneath her chin and raising her face to his. "Oh, yes, definitely boredom, I'd say." He gazed lazily down into her blue eyes, her lips slightly parted in surprise at his action. "Now why should such a beautiful girl look so bored, I wonder?"

"Maybe it's the people I seem to meet," Emily replied as smoothly and evenly as she could, trying to withdraw her chin from his firm, cool grasp. She didn't seem to be able to tear her eyes away from his wide, sensual mouth, while the touch of his fingers on her skin was having a most peculiar effect on her breathing. Emily had always prided herself on being in command of every situation, but she didn't somehow feel that she was in complete control at the moment.

"Touché," he laughed, and still firmly holding her chin, suddenly bent his head towards her soft red lips. She gasped as his hard mouth possessed hers in a firm, determined kiss.

"Well... really!" she protested, blushing with embarrassment as he finally let her go. "Do you... do you always go around treating people this way?"

"Oh, no." He gave her a wolfish grin. "But I must say it was thoroughly enjoyable! Maybe I should do it more often?"

"I... we... I mean, we haven't even been introduced..." she muttered lamely, furious with herself for not being able to think of anything better to say, and disturbed by the glint in the man's mocking grey eyes.

"No—we haven't have we? But I did have the distinct impression that you wished me to come over and talk to you. I just... er... decided to speed up our new acquaintance!" His eyes gleamed with amusement as she blushed and looked away.

"Well, I—I didn't mean..."

"Just let that be a lesson to you, my child. You should practice on someone of your own age. You're not old enough to play with the grown-ups yet!"

"How dare you! I..." Emily blurted out, almost choking with rage as the strange man continued to smile lazily down at her. Taking a deep breath, she struggled for a calmness she was very far from feeling.

"My dear old man," she drawled. "I left my childhood behind me a very long time ago. Although I'm pleased to say that I have yet to join you in senility!"

That should fix him, she thought balefully, gazing up into his handsome face. It was only now, standing so close to the strange, handsome man, that she noticed his dark hair was tipped with silver at the temples and that there were small lines around his wide grey eyes. He still couldn't be more than thirty-five, she thought, noticing that the infuriating man was grinning down at her, his shoulders shaking with silent laughter.

"Tell me," she added in a sweet voice which she hoped would annoy him, "are you really very old? I wouldn't have thought that you were much more than fifty-five myself."

To her fury and indignation, he gave a loud bark of laughter and raised her hand to his lips. "What an enchanting minx you are! I find you quite delightful."

"Which is more than I can say for you!" Emily snapped coldly, trying unsuccessfully to withdraw her hand. She sighed with relief as she saw Bob approaching.

"I might have known you'd move in on the only good looking woman here," Bob said in mock anger. "Go away and play with someone else, Ludo. I saw Miss Lambouchere first."

"What!" The man suddenly dropped her hand as if it were a hot brick. Startled, Emily looked up again into his face, surprised to see an expression of disgust cross his features, his warm smile replaced by a cold, hard frown.

"Haven't you two been introduced?" Bob said. "Okay, I'll do it properly. Miss Emily Lambouchere, this is Ludovic Vandenberg—a vile fellow and strictly not recommended for nice ladies!"

"I...er...I had gathered that," she murmured, glancing up through her eyelashes at the stranger who seemed suddenly distant and angry.

"I certainly had no idea I was talking to Miss Lambouchere of the Lambouchere Diamond Company. Are you intending to be out here for long?" he asked curtly in a hard, tight voice. "It wouldn't seem to be your usual stamping ground, would it? Surely San Tropez is the place for social butterflies at this time of the year?"

Emily gasped, feeling as if she had been hit by a hard blow to the solar plexus. God knows she was used to snide, envious remarks, but this man was being quite unnecessarily rude and for no good reason that she could see. Maybe he was joking—surely he must be? She essayed a brief smile. "Actually, I usually go to Marbella in July," she drawled lightly. "Followed by Scotland in August—of course."

"Of course!" His mouth became a hard, firm line of disapproval, his voice harsh and condemnatory. "Followed by hunting in the shires and then Saint Moritz in the winter, no doubt!" he sneered. "I can just see you in your house in Mayfair...."

"Knightsbridge," she corrected him coldly. He wasn't joking. This quite extraordinarily rude man was being deadly serious! Why? All she'd done was to look at him across the terrace.... She had...well, encouraged him to come over to her side; there was no doubt about that. She flushed slightly at the recollection. But—but it was he who had so rudely kissed her and now—now he was being damned insulting. Well, if he expected her to meekly accept his caustic virulence, he was in for a disappointment!

"I'm sorry to tell you, Mr. Vandenberg, that I don't hunt. As you are obviously a dedicated follower of the social season, I'm sure you will know that it's Acapulco in November, and that the Caribbean comes after Gstaad." Emily flashed him a brilliant smile. "Alas, Saint Moritz is definitely out these days. Strictly for the plebs, I'm afraid."

"I bet it is!" he snapped, his mouth set in a thin line, his tall body suddenly becoming stiff and menacing.

"Oh dear! You really don't seem to approve of me, Mr. Vandenberg," Emily murmured in a softly goading voice. "I wonder what I can have done to upset you?"

"I certainly don't approve of lazy social parasites who have nothing better to do than get their names in the gossip columns," he replied grimly, his cold hard grey eyes boring down into hers.

"Hang on a mo!" Bob interjected hastily, looking at them both in dismay. "There's no need to be so rude, Ludo," he said placatingly, looking around desperately for Andrew Sinclair. The way these two were squaring up to each other, it looked as if there was going to be blood on the floor any minute. It also looked as if they were all going to lose their jobs very shortly, thanks to this idiot. The woman had herself well under control, surprisingly well he thought, but she clearly wasn't going to take much more of Ludo's abuse.

"It's all right, Bob. If poor Mr. Vandenberg is stupid enough to believe everything he reads, especially out here in the back of beyond...." Emily shrugged dismissively, her face a cool mask of indifference, sharply at variance with her true feelings of suppressed fury. Who did this—this frightful man think he was? Her nails bit fiercely into the palm of her hand as she strove to maintain a glacial, contemptuous expression on her face. It was, she instinctively realised, proving far more infuriating to him than any display of anger on her part would have done.

"It would be a pleasure not to have to hear about you and your friends. Unfortunately, as I live part of the year in London, it is virtually impossible not to read about you and some of the other silly little rich girls who seem to enjoy making fools of themselves!" he said roughly, his voice heavy with contempt. "You are right, I don't approve of people like you and what you stand for."

Emily could feel her control slipping. The overwhelming urge to slap his handsome face was becoming almost more than she could resist. Never, in all her life, had anyone spoken to her the way he had. She might have had to put up with unkind, hurtful remarks before now, but never, absolutely never this—this arrant, insulting rudeness.

Emily threw back the heavy curtain of her silvery

blond hair. "You abysmally stupid, arrogant man! You know absolutely nothing about me, and even less about what I stand for," she retorted through clenched teeth. She could feel her body shaking with almost uncontrollable rage as she glared at his deeply tanned face with fierce loathing. "I don't suppose you can help letting blind prejudice cloud your judgement—but it isn't really very *grown-up*, is it?"

"Now," she added, taking a deep breath to steady herself and turning to Bob, "I really am bored to death with this stupid man. Let's go and find a drink, shall we?"

"Yeah...yeah, sure. Anything you say...." Bob clearly felt out of his depth as he allowed himself to be led away, their progress across the terrace being followed by Ludovic Vandenberg's hard gray eyes.

When they were out of sight around the corner of the house, Emily felt her rigid control give way and unable to stop herself from trembling violently, she sank down thankfully on to a stone bench. "Who...who in heaven is that—that man? I've never—never met anyone in all my life so—so incredibly rude!"

"I'm sure he didn't mean any of the...er...the things he said," Bob said, trying to reassure her.

"Oh yes he did!" she retorted bitterly, ashamed to see that her hands were shaking. "He meant every single, damned word. Who is he?"

"Well...." Bob took a gulp of his whisky. "Well, as you know, his name's Ludovic Vandenberg. He spends a lot of his time out here. He's a professor of zoology, or something like that. Anyway, he's normally down in the rain forests studying gorillas, except his film crew wanted some extra shots from around here."

"He makes films?"

"Well, sort of. He writes and makes films for TV. I'm told it's a great series all about gorillas, apes, chimps, etc. He's supposed to be a big authority on the subject, written books and all sorts of things."

"Ugh!" shuddered Emily. "Gorillas sound a bit grim."

"They're okay according to Ludo," Bob said. "He tells me they're much nicer than chimps or baboons for instance. Still, there's something funny about that guy...."

"Funny! What's funny about him? Hardly a laugh a minute, I'd have thought."

"Well...." He looked embarrassed. "It doesn't sound too good, it being your mine and all, but we had a Kaffir go kook a few weeks ago...."

"Kaffir...? Kook...?" Emily looked at him in puzzlement.

"One of the workers, a native worker—went berserk. Grabbed a gun from one of the guards and started shooting up the place. Killed a few of the other workers and...."

"How awful!"

Bob shrugged. "It happens sometimes. Anyway, Ludo and the team were in the middle of filming near this chap when he went off his rocker, and my word—I've never seen anything like it!"

"Like what?" demanded Emily.

"I couldn't believe my eyes—it all happened so quickly. One moment Ludo was standing still, the next minute he had grabbed a rifle from a guard and ran straight at the fellow, firing from the hip. It was difficult shooting because the man had got himself behind a large steel post, and naturally he began to fire back at Ludo."

"What happened then?" Emily found herself becoming interested, despite her strong dislike of the rude stranger.

"As soon as the worker started firing Ludo hit the deck, rolled over and over on the ground and shot the Kaffir stone dead, right through the heart."

"I don't see what's so special about that," she sniffed dismissively.

"What was so special was that Ludo was firing at the same time as he was rolling over the ground. Fantastic shooting, and really fast reactions."

"So...?"

"So—don't try and tell me that zoology professors normally do that sort of thing! Marines and paratroopers maybe, but even then they'd have a job to be as fast as he was. After he'd shot the fellow, Ludo just got up and dusted himself down, gave the gun back to the guard and went calmly back to filming." Bob finished his drink. "For the past few weeks he's also been warning people here that there's going to be trouble in the country. Like I said, there's something odd about him."

Emily stood up, brushing down her dress. "Well, I, for one, think that what's odd is that no one has ever taught him any manners! Do you think there's any food here? I'm starving."

"So am I," said Bob. "Let's go and see what Amy is providing tonight."

The rest of the evening passed peacefully. Andrew Sinclair and his fellow technicians didn't seem to be particularly worried about the political situation. Possibly feeling that what happened in the capital, Dekoa, was far removed from their enclosed world at the mine, Emily assumed. Her head was buzzing with the different names of the tribes, and the infighting which seemed to be going on between General Ngaro—soon to be king—and the leaders of the other three main tribes.

"You see, *mademoiselle*," said a young Frenchman, admiration of the beautiful woman shining out of his eyes, "it is like this...." Emily needed all her command of French to follow the convoluted tale.

"General Ngaro thinks he's Napoleon—and Napoleon had an army—*n'est-ce pas*? So he must have one, the Ouandan National Guard being very small. However, this is a poor country of only about two million inhabitants, most of whom live in small villages. So what does he do? He gets in touch with his good friend Robert Mugabe who rules Zimbabwe—which used to be Rhodesia—and he says, 'Have you got any men you can lend me?'"

Emily smiled. "I don't believe it!"

"It's true," he assured her. "Mugabe, of course, goes down on his knees and gives thanks to the good Lord. All those guerrillas who used to fight the whites—he can get rid of them at last! They have been a big headache to him, I can tell you. Now the fighting is over, they have nothing to do but fight and quarrel with each other. They do not know how to do anything else. So, he sends them up to General Ngaro here, *tout de suite*!"

"I don't see the problem. Surely everyone is happy, if what you say is right?" Emily sipped her drink and looked at the young Frenchman quizzically.

"Alas *mademoiselle*. General Ngaro only gives jobs in the government to members of his own tribe. Members of the other three tribes are angry, and although they hate each other of course, they have now come together to get rid of Ngaro and his new mercenaries. The rumour is that they have been out buying some mercenary troops of their own. Now, not only do the tribes hate each other, but the two mercenary armies would like nothing better than to get at each other's throats. So you see, it is a very inflammable situation."

"Nothing is really likely to happen, is it?" Emily asked anxiously.

"No, of course not. All will be quiet for the coronation—you will see. Monsieur Vandenberg, he spreads alarm, that is all."

I bet he does, thought Emily viciously. I'd like to spread some alarm all over him—I really would!

Her wish was granted rather sooner than she thought,

or indeed, desired. She was talking to Andrew Sinclair, making arrangements for him to pick her up the next morning for a tour of the mine. "Now I really must go," she said. "It has been a lovely evening, but I'm a little tired."

"I'm sure you are," he said sympathetically. "The weather at this time of year can be trying, to say the least. I'll just get the car and run you back to your bungalow."

"Please, don't bother," she said. "I'm sure that you shouldn't leave your own party, not before the rest of your guests go, anyway. Possibly there's some young man who can drop me off...?"

"There's no need to worry," said a voice behind her. The dark, rich voice she had come to hate. "I'm going past the guest bungalow and will be happy to give Miss Lambouchere a lift."

"There's no need to trouble yourself," Emily said hurriedly.

"It's no trouble," he said, putting a firm hand on her arm. "In fact, it will be a pleasure!" he purred.

"That's kind of you Ludo," said Andrew. "I'll just go and get Miss Lambouchere's overalls for her tour of the mine tomorrow. I won't be a minute."

"Let go of my arm this minute, you ghastly man!" she hissed, watching Andrew Sinclair's retreating figure.

"Oh no—you might run away, and I don't intend that you should," he answered firmly.

"Really Mr. Vandenberg—this is too ridiculous. I just want to leave quietly...."

"Of course you do," he replied soothingly. She glanced quickly up at him. He sounded much calmer than he had earlier in the evening, but there was a disturbing glitter in his eyes that troubled her.

"We—we have nothing to say to each other. Nothing that hasn't already been said, that is!"

"Oh Emily! It is Emily, isn't it? What a lovely old-fashioned name—it doesn't seem to suit you, somehow." His voice was rich with ironic amusement.

"My name is none of your business! Please let me go." She tried to pull her arm away, but his grip only tightened. "Please," she gasped as his fingers bit into her flesh, "you're hurting me!" Where's Bob? Why doesn't somebody rescue me from this madman? She looked around in desperation.

"Stop struggling and then I won't hurt you," he replied in a maddeningly calm voice, as the manager returned with a white garment over his arm.

"Mr. Sinclair...I think that I...." The fingers bit harder into her arm and Emily was hard put to not cry out in pain. I won't give him the satisfaction, she thought, gritting her teeth.

"Are you all right, Miss Lambouchere?" Andrew Sinclair looked anxiously at the woman's pale cheeks.

"She's fine." Then Ludovic Vandenberg asked her softly, "Aren't you, Emily?"

Emily looked around at the other guests who were gazing in their direction, waiting for them to go. There was absolutely no point in creating a scene, and she seemed to have no alternative but to accompany this mentally deranged man whose hand seemed to be made of steel.

"Yes...yes, I'm fine. Thank you, Mr. Sinclair. I'll see you tomorrow."

Ludovic Vandenberg relaxed his grip slightly as they walked down the path towards his vehicle, but he still kept a firm hold of her arm. Emily walked silently beside him, seething with fury.

"Up you get," he said, opening the door of what seemed in the darkness to be a ramshackle vehicle.

"Up where?" she snapped. "You can't seriously expect me to travel in this...this...heap of scrap iron."

"Not exactly a Mercedes or a Porsche, I grant you,"

he said. "But some of us 'plebs' are happy to travel in a Land Rover. Especially over the local terrain." Without any warning he swept her up in his arms and roughly dumped her on the seat in one fluid movement, before slamming the door shut and going around to the other side of the vehicle.

She sat where he had so unceremoniously placed her, almost rigid with fury. "I hope there is some point to this stupid charade," she cried angrily.

"Of course." He started the engine and drove away from the Sinclairs. "I wanted to talk to you—privately. I have two things to say to you. The first is to apologise for letting my prejudices against silly little rich girls show so clearly, and the second is to warn you, very strongly, not to stay in Ouanda a day longer than you need to. The situation here is very dangerous indeed."

Emily gasped with fury, and then took a deep breath in an effort to calm herself down. She just wanted to get back to the bungalow, and she had no intention of indulging in a slanging match with someone who was, without doubt, quite the rudest and most unpleasant man she had ever met.

"Did you hear what I said?"

"I heard."

"Then I hope you will accept my apology and heed my warning." His voice grated harshly in the darkness as he brought the Land Rover to a stop outside the bungalow.

Emily's head felt as if it was bursting as she struggled to keep silent. It was no good; the effect this man was having on her was more than flesh and blood could be expected to stand. "I—I will leave Ouanda exactly when and how I please," she cried in a high, breathless voice she hardly recognised as her own. "What is more, I'm certainly not accepting your so-called apology! And—and don't you ever—ever again put a foot on any property belonging to the Lambouchere company. Because you'd better believe me when I tell you that I shall give orders for you to be arrested immediately! If it was possible I'd also arrange for you to be shot on sight!" she added viciously.

"Trying to bludgeon me with your wealth, Miss Lambouchere?" He gave a dry bark of sardonic laughter.

"You're so damn right! It is only when I have to deal with such—such crassly boring members of the proletariat—such as yourself—that I truly appreciate the joy, and the power, of being stinking rich!"

"My God, you're a little vixen!" he hissed in the darkness beside her, grabbing her arm and holding it in a vicelike grip.

"You seem to be given to violence—as well as bad manners!" she gasped, wincing at the pain he was inflicting. "You've already hurt my other arm. Are you trying to make it a matched set?"

With a strangled oath he let go of her arm. "Let me tell you something," she cried, frantically searching for the door handle. "I grew up in a hard school, Mr. Vandenberg. You've no idea how hard. And I don't mean the kind where you learn your ABC either. You seem to think you're so tough—hah!" She gave a tremulous laugh. "You're nothing but a—a bag of wind! Full of brute force and bloody ignorance and—and let me out of this damned vehicle—at once!" she added with a sob in her voice.

Cursing violently under his breath, he got out of the Land Rover and came around to open her door. "Come on," he growled, "out you get."

"I would if I could," she shouted in furious exasperation, "but there seems to be some sort of pole across the opening, and I can't...I can't get my foot over it."

"Oh, for heaven's sake!" he exclaimed. "It's only the camera tripod." Reaching into the Land Rover, he clasped her waist firmly and pulled her roughly out of the vehicle. Emily stumbled as she felt her feet touch the ground, throwing her arms forward in a wild attempt to regain her balance. Less than a second later she was in his arms.

They looked at each other in shocked surprise, his arms tightening about her slim, soft figure. *"No!"* she gasped as his face came down towards hers, blotting out the moonlight.

It was an angry, savage kiss, deeply insulting in its violation of her senses. Emily's fists beat helplessly against his broad chest as she fought and struggled to escape the iron grip of his arms, the scorching heat of his mouth.

Only when she was exhausted by her efforts to free herself, no longer able to fight his superior strength, did he lift his mouth from her bruised lips. Emily's eyes were brimming over with tears as she shook her head distractedly, trying to clear her dazed and shocked mind.

"I—I..." she croaked, unable to make any sense of her disordered and chaotic thoughts.

"Silent at last, Miss Lambouchere?" he murmured thickly. "Well, that makes a pleasant change, doesn't it?"

"Let me go, you—you beast!" she cried hoarsely, trembling in his arms.

"Certainly." Ludovic Vandenberg released the shaken woman and leant casually against the Land Rover as he watched her stumble up the path to the bungalow. Emily opened the door and turned to face his lounging figure.

"I hate you...I hate you!" she screamed. "I never want to see you again, never...never...never! And even then, it would be too soon!" she yelled, slamming the front door loudly behind her, his sardonic laugh ringing in her ears.

CHAPTER TWO

THE MORNING SUN flooded into the bedroom, falling on the form of the woman sleeping in the big double bed beneath the white cloud of a mosquito net. Her long brown legs lay in a graceful pose, the ash-blond hair covering her face, her head buried in her arms. It was very quiet, apart from a fly which buzzed lazily by the window. The birds sang softly outside, a faint breeze stirring the branches of the trees surrounding the bungalow.

The peaceful scene was suddenly shattered by two large explosions some way away, followed by a third somewhat nearer. Emily's eyes jerked open and she sat up with a start. What in the hell was that, she thought bemused, rubbing her drowsy eyes and trying to remember where she was. The birds resumed their singing as quiet descended once again, and she rolled over to look at her small travelling clock on the bedside table.

Ten o'clock. *You've overslept*, she told herself, and then shrugged. She wasn't going to be picked up for her tour of the diamond mine until 11:30 that morning, so it really didn't matter. What did matter, she thought as she tried to clear her dry throat, was that her request to be woken with a cup of tea at nine o'clock hadn't been obeyed.

She'd made it quite clear to the resident housekeeper and the three other servants who looked after the bungalow. Although she obviously had not been able to converse in their native tongue, they had seemed perfectly capable of understanding French which, after the hundred years or so of French colonial rule, was the lingua franca of the country.

She got out of bed and ringing the bell for a servant, went into the adjoining bathroom to wash, and brush her teeth. How she hated sleeping pills. Grimacing at herself in the mirror, Emily splashed her face with cold water. They always left her feeling so muzzy in the morning. However, they did ensure a good night's sleep, allowing her to stagger from one boring day to another. She had hoped that at least out here in Ouanda, life might have proved to be more entertaining. But it hadn't. Not at all.

Emily scowled, as she tied the cord of her silk dressing gown with angry fingers. That man last night...damn him! He'd really got under her skin. Who in the hell did he think he was...? Some awful professor of zoology, having the nerve to treat her the way he had.... He was nothing but a disgusting animal! She banged the bathroom door behind her in a sudden spasm of rage, going over to the wall to ring again for a servant.

Emily sat down to brush her hair. The expensively cut and even more expensively straightened silvery blond hair was proving difficult to control in the humid heat of equatorial Africa. Naturally very curly, Emily had never thought that it suited the smooth image she had painstakingly created as a carapace to protect herself. The armour that anyone moving amongst the jet set needed to survive. So, she wore her hair straight, touching her shoulders, or she would if she could only stop it curling in this heat, she thought in annoyance.

After waiting ten minutes, and there still being no appearance of a servant, she got up and went to the door. What a dump, she thought, scowling as she wandered through the cool rooms. Badly furnished, hideous colours, and no damn service. Emily's bad temper increased as it became obvious that the bungalow was devoid of all human habitation. When she thought of the army of servants back in London, eating their heads off, with precious little work to do . . . . This is ridiculous, she thought. There must be somebody here, surely?

But there wasn't. The kitchen, when she eventually found it, was spotlessly clean and empty. "Oh great!" she grumbled aloud, looking round for a kettle. At least she could make a pot of tea, although anything more than that was beyond her. Never having had to lift a finger in her life, meant that she had no idea how to even boil an egg, and she certainly didn't intend to start now!

Later, looking down at her cup of tea, Emily's anger at the absence of the servants had simmered down somewhat. It didn't really matter a damn, she thought glumly. In fact, very little mattered these days. All in all, it seemed as if the trip out to this bleak country was definitely one of her worst mistakes, although the invitation to attend the coronation of General Ngaro had seemed such a godsend at the time. Anything that would take her out of London—out of circulation— would have been welcomed with open arms. Anything to get away from the scandal which had engulfed her.

Whatever had possessed her to get engaged to James Wooldridge? Emily frowned, trying to remember just why she had accepted his proposal, after having turned down so many in the past. She sighed and sipped her tea.

It had been a long boring weekend in May, she remembered. She'd been invited to join a house party in Hampshire, and it had rained every day. James had offered to drive her back to London and on the way he had proposed, yet again. It must have been sheer boredom that prompted her to say yes—there was no real reason why she should have accepted him otherwise.

James Wooldridge, Eton and the Guards, had recently joined his father's firm, Wooldridge Life Insurance. Sir Bryan Wooldridge, James' father, had been rather a poppet, she had thought, when he had greeted their engagement with delight.... What a fool you were, she castigated herself. What a stupid fool!

Some of her friends had lifted their eyebrows, and been surprised at her choice. "Darling!" Maria Reeves had said, "he's awfully sweet, of course. But do you really think he's one of us?" Maria had wrinkled her nose. "Trade—and all that sort of thing, *darling*!"

"Maria," Emily had retorted, with a faint smile, as a heavy lorry went by in the street outside, "that rumbling I hear must be your father spinning in his grave! He did make his fortune from selling boiled sweets, didn't he—*darling*?"

Possibly the chief virtue that James possessed in her eyes was that he didn't want to marry her for her money. Not only did his father, Sir Bryan Wooldridge, own the insurance company that bore his name, but he was chairman and a large stockholder of many city institutions. The wedding was set for the end of July, and after all, getting married would be a new experience. She had felt impelled to try and do something with her life. The vacuous and futile round of mindless pleasure seeking was becoming almost more than she could bear.

Emily didn't bother with the administration of her capital funds; there was a large block of real estate in the city which was filled with employees engaged on doing just that. So she failed, therefore, to understand the significance of the dramatic rise in the shares of the Wooldridge financial empire when their engagement was officially announced. The first intimation of all not being well, had come on a flight back to London from Paris, where she had been having a fitting for her trousseau.

There had been nothing to read, until the man next to her handed her a copy of The Economist magazine. Flicking through the articles, she had suddenly seen her name spread across the centre pages: "Lambouchere Millions Save City Firm."

Startled, she had read on to discover that it was only the promise of her marriage to James, which was keeping Sir Bryan's company afloat. There had been heavy overcapitalization and cash-flow problems, as well as threats of investigation by the fraud squad, if what she understood of the financial jargon was correct.

Arriving back in London she had gone immediately to see James. He had smiled sheepishly as he reluctantly confirmed the article in the magazine. "There's no point in hiding it from you, Emily. It's not going to make any difference to us, surely?"

"This isn't the Victorian age, James, and even I have heard of the Married Woman's Property Act. Why in the world should you think that I'm going to hand over my money to you and your father?" she had asked angrily.

"But you love me, Emily," he protested, looking sulky. "You know you do. Why else should you have agreed to marry me?"

"Why else indeed?" she sighed. With sudden clarity she had looked past his blond good looks, noting for the first time the weak chin, the pale, vapid blue eyes shifting under her direct gaze. "James, I don't love you and you don't love me either—just the idea of financial salvation."

"I say! That's going a bit far, Emily...." James' cheeks were tinged with pink as her words hit home.

"It's not your fault," she shrugged wearily. "I should never have accepted your proposal." She paused, looking at him intently for a moment. "Frankly, James," she said slowly, "I don't think a lifetime, or even a few years of your company, would be worth what I would have to pay."

"Emily! You can't mean it...."

"Indeed I do," she had retorted, rising to her feet. "Please tell your father that the—the 'deal' is off. Goodbye James."

"Come back, Emily!" James had shouted down the

stairs as she left his flat in Mayfair. She had not even glanced back, despite the note of entreaty in his voice, as she got in her car and drove away to stay with friends in Yorkshire for the weekend.

It had been lovely weather and she had stayed on for a week, enjoying the June sunshine. It was only on her return to her London house that the full import of her broken engagement had begun to hit her. Emily's home was surrounded by corps of pressmen, and she had had to fight her way inside, running a gauntlet of shouted questions.

"What's going on?" she had demanded on reaching the sanctuary of the large inner hall.

Wilson, her butler, had shrugged. "It seems, madam," he said in sepulchral tones, "that Sir Bryan Wooldridge has committed suicide, and his firm has collapsed, owing people a great deal of money."

"Oh no!" Emily blanched. "Oh...how dreadful!"

Just how dreadful, she had found out. There were apparently thousands of small investors who had lost all their savings. Encouraged by newspaper headlines such as "Heiress Rats on Fiancé" and "Withdrawal of Lambouchere Fortune Kills Insurance Firm," she had even had pickets parading up and down outside her house asking for their money back.

She had gone to see her trustees in the city, to see if there was any way she could help the small savers who had lost everything, but they had refused to understand her feeling that she had an obligation to do something. They had merely congratulated her on her astuteness in withdrawing from a sinking ship in the nick of time, turning a deaf ear to her request.

In the midst of her nightmare, the invitation to the coronation of General Ngaro in Ouanda, had come as the only welcome chink of light amidst the encircling gloom. She knew that she must be a figure of social ridicule amongst her friends, until the dust died down anyway. She had to escape from London, and Ouanda seemed to provide the answer. So she had accepted, making plans to go on afterwards to stay with some acquaintances in South Africa. That should keep her out of England for some months, and hopefully most people would have forgotten everything by the time she returned.

Emily shook herself and finished her cup of tea. It was no good looking back. Regretting the fact that she had ever accepted James' proposal wasn't going to make things any better. She stood up and walked through the empty rooms, the silence beginning to disturb her. The only sound was the flat slap of her slippers on the cool marble floor. Something was disturbing her, and she couldn't think what... of course—the birds! The birds had stopped singing and—and it all seemed a bit odd. She went over and lifted the receiver of the telephone. It seemed to be working, so she dialled the manager's office at the mine. Puzzled, she let it ring for some time before replacing the receiver. Surely, at this time of the day, there should be someone there.

She wandered slowly back into her bedroom, the first stirrings of unease beginning to cloud her mind. Shrugging, Emily decided to have a shower, the heat of the day already causing her to perspire.

Feeling refreshed from the shower's cool spray she walked back into the bedroom, trying to think what to do. There was at least an hour before Andrew Sinclair came to fetch her for her tour of the mine, and it was far too hot to climb into the heavy white overalls one minute before she had to. The only casual clothes she had brought with her were a pair of faded denim shorts and a thin, sleeveless lawn blouse. The Ouandan Embassy had provided her with a list of her engagements during her visit, and as it was a fairly crowded schedule she had decided to buy any sports wear she might need when she got to South Africa.

She got dressed slowly in front of the full length mirror, regarding herself with critical eyes. Like so many beautiful women, Emily was dissatisfied with the way she looked. Really, she thought gloomily, my only claim to attraction is my legs: "legs which are so long they seem to start under her shoulders" as one gossip columnist had put it. It certainly isn't your bust, she told herself, as she did up the thin blouse. How she had wept at boarding school when she had been forced to wear a bra, long before any of the other girls in her dormitory. Well, it was much too hot to wear one at the moment, she thought, thanking her stars that her breasts were firm even if she considered them too large. They still felt sore from having been crushed so hard and ruthlessly against *that man's* chest last night.

Her face darkened. She still felt furiously angry with Ludovic Vandenberg. My goodness he had a nerve! He seemed to think he was God's gift to women, and how....

There was a sudden roar of an aircraft overhead which cut abruptly into her thoughts. So loud it had to be practically touching the trees, she thought in panic as she flinched and ran to the window. She could see nothing, but then heard the plane return, still flying very low, the roar of its engines filling her ears. There was a deafening rattle on the roof, like pebbles being dropped one after another.

Emily's chief reaction was one of anger. "What in the name of heaven's going on?" she shouted loudly, walking out of her room, through the hall and on to the terrace. No servants, aeroplanes beating up her bungalow.... Someone should bring some law and order to this crazy country, and darn fast! She kicked a pebble on the terrace in irritation and was surprised when it clanked as it rolled away from her.

For the first time since coming out on to the terrace, she looked around her. The stone pots which held flowering shrubs had all been smashed—one after another in a straight line, she noticed, and bending down to pick up the pebble she saw that it looked remarkably like a flattened bullet.

"How odd," she muttered, startled out of her self-pity by the strange happenings of the morning. She walked on to the lawn, shading her eyes from the sun as she looked back at the roof of the bungalow. There was a neat line of holes right across one side.

For heaven's sake, she thought in shocked amazement, that—that aeroplane was shooting up the bungalow! Whatever for? The question remained unanswered as the birds resumed their chirping amidst the tall trees.

With trembling legs she sank down on a stone bench and looked about her. It was all so—so eerie, she thought, shuddering apprehensively. The quiet peaceful garden, the deserted house...suddenly they had become frightening and she felt lonely and afraid. "You can't sit here all day," she muttered resolutely, gritting her teeth and forcing herself to get up and walk down the path to the dirt road at the end of the garden. The morning fog still hadn't lifted down in the valley; curling wisps of mist swirled at the far end of the road. Shading her eyes, she strove to see more clearly what seemed to be a vehicle parked about three hundred yards away.

It's no good staying here, she thought decisively. The telephone doesn't work, and I haven't any transport. Maybe there's someone in the car who can help me, or if it's empty, maybe I can use it to get help. Having made her decision, Emily strode purposefully off down the road which led, she remembered, to the mine.

She was almost upon the vehicle, some sort of Jeep, when she saw an oddly shaped bundle of clothes on the road. She went over to investigate it, and she staggered back in shock, shaking and trembling at what she saw. A black man lay crumpled face downwards on the road, the back of his white shirt punctured by large holes from which issued an ever-widening stream of blood. There was no doubt that he was very dead indeed.

Emily felt her gorge rise, and feeling faint she backed away, stumbling over her feet which were suddenly as heavy as lead. Gasping, she turned and ran crying with shock to the Jeep whose windscreen had been shattered, her shoes crunching on the pieces of glass lying all over the road.

Andrew Sinclair sat in the driving seat, bent oddly over the driving wheel, his head turned away from her.

"Andrew!" she cried in terror, "are you all right?" There was no reply, except for the buzzing of flies, as she reached into the vehicle to try and help him sit up. Panting, Emily pulled and kicked at the door, but it was jammed fast and she couldn't move it. She swiftly ran around the Jeep, wrenching open the passenger door.

"Oh, it can't be...!" she moaned in fright and horror at what she saw. Andrew lay propped upon the wheel facing her, his open eyes staring blindly at her from a face that was the grey colour of putty. She had to swallow rapidly several times, before she could force herself to get into the vehicle and try to move him off the wheel. Eventually she managed to prop him back on the seat, and saw that he was indeed dead. A line of bullet holes had riddled his body, in the same way as the man lying on the road.

She began to shake, her teeth rattling loudly as she got out of the Jeep. Moaning and whimpering, she looked around in desperation. What could she do? Where should she go? The thoughts ran like mice in her brain, scurrying here and there. She felt as cold as ice, despite the heat of the day, and she couldn't stop herself shaking.

It was some moments before she realised that what she had thought was a whirring in her head, was the sound of a car approaching from the direction of the

mine. "Let it stop...please God, let it stop..." she
whimpered, running towards the approaching vehicle,
waving her hands desperately in the air, her eyes practically blinded by tears.

The vehicle screeched to a halt, and a man jumped
out as the terrified woman ran screaming up to him,
her eyes wide with terror. His hands went out to catch
her, bringing her to a scrambling halt.

"Thank—thank goodness it's you!" she cried, gazing up feverishly at Ludovic Vandenberg. All thoughts
of their encounter last night were absent, as she clung
thankfully to him, crying and shaking like a leaf.

"Calm down Emily. What's the matter?" he asked
in a firm voice.

"The Jeep...the aeroplane...the bullets hit the
bungalow...and there's a man on the road..." she
babbled, pointing to the Jeep behind her. "Oh, God
help me!" she screamed. "They're all dead! The blood
and flies...."

"Come on, Emily, pull yourself together," he said,
roughly shaking her shoulders. But she could only cry
and scream out incoherently, firmly in the grip of hys-
terical terror.

Ludovic raised his arm and slapped her twice across
the face. "I'm sorry—but it was necessary," he said in
a harsh voice as Emily's head rocked back at the blows.
She gave a few hiccuping sobs, before becoming silent
and white faced, staring blindly at him from terrified
blue eyes.

"Stay here—I'll be back in a minute," he said
firmly, leaning her stiff, trembling body against the
Land Rover. Emily watched him stride off towards the
Jeep, and suddenly feeling sick she ran frantically to
the side of the road.

She was still retching desperately, when Ludovic returned grim faced from his inspection of the Jeep. "Are
you all right?" he asked, not unkindly, as she stood

trembling beside the ditch. She nodded dumbly, allow-ing herself to be led unresisting back to the Land Rover. He helped her into the passenger seat and then got in and drove them back up the road to the bungalow.

She was trembling, rigid with fear as he lifted her out and carried her into the house, smashing open the door of her bedroom with his foot, before placing her on the bed.

"I've never seen a d-dead m-man b-b-before," she stuttered, her teeth chattering so hard that she found it difficult to formulate the words.

"Never mind about that, Emily. We have more im-portant things to do, now." He looked down at the trem-bling girl. "Emily . . . ? Emily! Are you listening to me?" He shook her shoulder roughly. His voice seemed to be coming from a long way off, she thought as his words gradually began to penetrate her dazed mind.

"Y-yes . . ." she nodded, like a doll. "Yes—I'm lis-tening. . . ." She could hear her teeth chattering in the silence, and a muscle seemed to be aching at the back of her jaw.

"Right. You have ten minutes, no longer, to get your things together. Only the bare essentials, I'm afraid. . . ."

"Don't leave me . . . !" she cried in terror, leaping off the bed and clutching at his arm as he turned to leave the room. "Please, please don't leave me," she pleaded.

He looked down into her large blue eyes, filled with tears. "It's all right, Emily," he said gently, brushing the hair away from her forehead. "I'm not going to leave you, but I must go and push the Jeep off the road and remove any trace of the incident. I don't want any-one to stop and investigate what has happened—it's too near this bungalow."

"You promise to come back?" she asked anxiously, still clinging tightly to his arm.

He gave a dry bark of laughter. "I promise. I have

instructions to look after you, so there is no doubt that I will return. Just be ready in ten minutes." He left the room with purposeful strides.

Emily was sitting huddled on the bed, having been sick again, when he returned. She was surrounded by open suitcases, all quite empty.

"Good Lord, Emily!" he said loudly. "Why aren't you ready? I said we only had ten minutes.... Of all the crass, stupid...!"

"Don't talk to me like that!" she shouted wildly, jumping to her feet. "Pack up, you said. Only—only the bare essentials you said...." Emily faltered, her large blue eyes widening as she realised she was going to be sick again. Frantically she dashed for the bathroom.

"You—you never said where we were—were going," she gasped, leaning over the basin as Ludovic roughly and with ill-concealed impatience bathed her forehead with a cold flannel. "The—the bare essentials for what...?" Emily shivered, allowing herself to be led back into the bedroom. "I mean...do I take my—my Balenciaga dresses, or—or the Saint Laurent separates...or what?" she wailed, collapsing on the bed.

"Oh Emily!" he leant laughing against the door. "Balenciaga and Saint Laurent are out this week, I'm afraid! When I said the bare essentials, I meant just that; you stupid girl. Brush, comb, and more or less what you are wearing—rather more if possible," he said, sliding his eyes down her long bare legs topped by the minuscule pair of shorts.

"But I—I haven't got any more casual clothes, only the ones I'm wearing," she moaned, sitting hunched on the bed in misery and trying desperately to stop her limbs from trembling.

Ludovic groaned with impatience at the sight of the dejected girl, and went swiftly around the room with a small, empty case, scooping up anything that looked remotely useful. He disappeared into the bathroom, and reappeared with her sponge-bag which he threw into the case. "Anything else?" he demanded. "We must go now."

"No, I don't...oh, heavens," she cried. "My—my passport and jewellery!" She scrambled off the bed and went to a cupboard, removing a green lizard case.

"There's women for you," he barked sardonically. "Rome may be burning, but they would never leave their jewellery behind—oh, no!"

"Where—where are we going?" she cried, as he took her hand and led her swiftly from the house. "Just where are you—you taking me...?"

"What in the hell does it matter?" he asked angrily. "You aren't planning to stay here, I take it?" Ludovic threw her bag into the back of the Land Rover.

Emily looked at him in sharp alarm. Despite the attack by the aeroplane, the bungalow and the quiet garden were known factors. This—this man Ludovic...he was apparently going to take her somewhere—it could be anywhere for all she knew....

"Come on," Ludovic snapped impatiently, holding the door open for her.

"No! I...no, I won't. I'm not going—going anywhere," she cried breathlessly through chattering teeth. "Not—not unless I know where I'm going. I—I don't trust you...."

"Don't drive me to violence, Emily, or you will be very sorry!" He ground his teeth in frustration.

"I—I don't care what you do to me, I'm—I'm not frightened," she cried, knowing that her show of bravado was betrayed by her trembling. "You—you could be kidnapping me, for all I know...." she added, with a sob.

"Heaven preserve me...." he muttered, and then gave a deep sigh. "Look," he said, letting go of the car door and grasping her firmly by the shoulders. "It's a very simple choice that you have, Emily. You can live, or you can die. If you stay here, you will die. The mercenary troops are still looting down at the mine, but it won't be long before they come along this way. And then you will indeed die, and it will not be a pleasant death. Do you understand what I'm saying?''

Emily could only stare up at him, her eyes wide with horror.

"I personally believe that everyone has a right to choose their own fate. Unfortunately, in your case, it is not a decision that I can allow you to make. I have very firm instructions to see that you are taken to a place of safety, which under the present circumstances means out of Ouanda.''

"What—what do you mean? Oh ... !'' Ludovic swept her up in his arms and she found herself in the Land Rover, the door slammed and the vehicle reversing out on to the dirt road, before she had time to collect her wits.

"How are we going to—to get out of Ouanda? And—and *what* circumstances ... ?'' she asked as the Land Rover sped down the road, completely bewildered by the speed of events.

"Shut up, Emily,'' he said firmly. "I am deciding what to do and trying to plan how we shall do it. So stop asking inane questions, and just say your prayers that my decisions are right. Because if they're not—neither of us will survive to see tomorrow.''

Sitting huddled on the hard seat, her shaking hands clasped tightly between her knees, Emily glanced quickly sideways at Ludovic as he drove at top speed down the bumpy dirt-track road. Looking at his hard, firm, handsome profile, she shivered apprehensively. She was, she realised, completely and helplessly at the mercy and in the hands of this strange man, who had clearly shown that he actively despised her and all she stood for.

CHAPTER THREE

EMILY CLIMBED WEARILY DOWN from her seat and stretched her long legs, thankful that they seemed to have stopped, at last. Ludovic had allowed her a five-minute stop some hours ago, to answer a call of nature, but apart from that they had been travelling constantly since this morning. He had passed her a bottle of water from time to time and had produced some sandwiches and fruit for lunch. However, nothing would persuade him to halt their rapid progress, until he had put as much distance as possible between himself and the troops he had talked about.

After an hour of silence, she had ventured to ask him a question, but after being told to "shut up" again, there had been no further communication between them. Until, just as the sun was setting, he had drawn to a halt and announced that this was where they would spend the night.

Emily looked around her. Ludovic had parked the Land Rover in a thin belt of trees on the edge of a wide grass plain which seemed to stretch as far as the eye could see. It looked as if there were mountains in the background, but in the fading light it was difficult to be sure. A damp fog seemed to float over the grassland; even as she watched it grew thicker, obliterating most of the view.

The Land Rover itself was an amazing-looking vehicle. Painted in brown and green camouflage colours, it was far longer than any she had seen before. It was long enough for someone to be able to lie down in the back, she thought, looking in through one of the dusty windows at the benches which ran down either side of the vehicle. A heavy rack of stainless steel protruded out from the roof over the bonnet, held up by thick steel poles welded to the front bumper. The rack was tightly packed with jerrycans, for petrol she presumed. With two spare wheels, one over the boot and one fixed to the rear door, the Land Rover looked the tough vehicle it undoubtedly was.

"Come on, Emily. Come along and make yourself useful," Ludovic called from behind her. She stiffly and wearily turned to see what he wanted. "Scout through the woodland and see if you can find some firewood—nothing too large," he warned her. "Come on!" he said again, "Chop, chop!"

She scowled at him before going reluctantly into the wood, the tall trees and the dense undergrowth impeding her way. It wasn't easy to see where she was going in the quickly gathering darkness. Twice she fell headlong on the ground, tripping over fallen branches. Sitting on a tree trunk, dazed from the second fall, she heard him call impatiently from the Land Rover. "If he says 'come along Emily' once more," she muttered angrily as her fingers gingerly felt a graze on her forehead, "I'll damn well brain him with one of these logs!"

"That's a poor effort," he said disparagingly, looking at the small bundle of firewood she had managed to find. "That certainly won't be much use to cook with, will it?"

"How in the hell do I know how much wood you need?" she grumbled, angrily throwing the pile on the ground.

"Pick them up, and stack them tidily by the circle of stones I've made on the ground over there," he said in a firm voice. "Do it!" he commanded sternly, as she hesitated, longing to defy him. She glared at him with hatred before turning away to carry out his order.

"That's better," he said approvingly, when she had finished building the pile. "Now, you've got brushwood and some leaves there, plus a box of matches. So you can get on with lighting a fire."

Emily opened her mouth to tell him to get lost. Light a fire? She'd never lit a fire in her life, and she certainly wasn't going to start learning now—thank you very much! Glancing at his face, she closed her lips with a snap. The patronising swine. He knew damn well she had no idea what to do. Well, she'd show him! It couldn't be too difficult—not if little boy scouts could manage it.

"Remember that a fire needs air, Emily," he called cheerfully over his shoulder, as he went back to the Land Rover and got out the radio transmitter from its secret compartment. Clamping on the headphones, he began to pass on the required information.

Emily squatted down, concentrating on her problem. She'd light this damn fire—even if she died in the attempt! Never, in all her life had she ever met a man she hated so much as Ludovic. How could she have possibly thought he was handsome? She must have been out of her mind! She clenched her teeth, trying to prevent the tears of frustration from falling down her cheeks as the logs of wood resolutely refused to catch fire. What had he said about fires needing air...? She started again, and by much dint of huffing and blowing, managed to get the leaves and brushwood alight.

"Not bad, Emily," he said, on his return. "In fact, a very credible first attempt."

She stood up, contemplating the small fire with disapproval. "There's no need to be so damn condescending. It's a pathetic attempt, as well you know," she snapped irritably. "But I'll do better next time, just you see if I don't!"

He looked at the girl regarding him so defiantly. The smoke had caused her eyes to water, the tears leaving tracks down her dusty cheeks. He tried not to smile, thinking that she seemed more of an angry, frustrated child, than a grown woman.

"I'm sure you will," he said soothingly. "Now, it's getting late, so we had better have something to eat."

With deft, economical movements, he prepared a simple supper for them from a store of tins he had in the Land Rover, and it wasn't long before he passed her a plate of stew and potatoes.

"Oh...I can't," she said in a small voice. "I'm sorry, I really can't."

"I'm afraid I don't have Escoffier's touch, but you must eat it up just the same," he said firmly.

"I'm sorry, Ludovic, it's...it's nothing to do with the cooking, really it isn't," she assured him. "I—I just couldn't face anything at all."

"I'm sorry too, Emily. But I'm afraid that you must eat the food. I really can't be expected to look after someone who doesn't help themselves to keep fit and well. Start eating!" he commanded her. "Now!"

"You can't make me," she snapped furiously, looking with distaste at the food and throwing him a glare of dislike.

"Oh yes I can, so don't be so stupid," he laughed dismissively. "I'll ram it down your throat if I have to—so eat!"

She looked at his stern impersonal expression, his hard grey eyes, and shuddered as she reluctantly began to eat her stew. "That's better," he said, "and my name's Ludo by the way."

She studiously ignored him, as she ploughed her way doggedly through the food he had given her. By the time he passed her a cup of coffee she had to reluctantly admit that she did feel very much better.

"That—that wasn't too bad...er...Ludo," she grudgingly admitted. "I...er...you were right, I suppose. It would be stupid not to eat."

"Quite a handsome apology—under the circumstances!" Ludo laughed briefly and then looked at her more seriously. "Now Emily, I must know whether you've had all the necessary inoculations, etc. Malaria is a very real possibility in this country—not to mention sleeping sickness!"

Emily stared at him resentfully. "I'm not entirely a fool, even if you think I am," she replied coldly. "I felt like a pincushion before I left London, full of antitetanus, typhoid, yellow fever and heaven knows what else. Before you ask," she added, "I've taken a course of antimalaria tablets, although no one mentioned sleeping sickness."

"They wouldn't! The Ouandan Government like to pretend that the tsetse fly has been eliminated from the country, but unfortunately it hasn't. I'll give you a dose of diamidine, which should hold good for sixty days...."

"Sixty days?" Emily's mouth dropped open. "There's no way I'm staying in this godforsaken country for sixty days!"

"Of course not," Ludo's voice was soothing. "However, we must all be good little boy scouts and 'be prepared' mustn't we?" He grinned at her and although she tried to preserve a stony countenance, she found herself giving him a faint, if reluctant smile in return.

"Can I...er...please ask you a question? Well, two questions, actually. Without having my head bitten off?" she said, deciding to take advantage of his better humour.

"Ask away. I'll answer them if I can," he replied, making a pile of their dirty plates.

"You—you said something about mercenary troops and looting, at—at the mine, and how you'd had instructions about me? I—I don't understand it at all."

"We'll talk about the mine later," he said firmly. "I'm not prevaricating. We'll discuss it when we have more time, okay?" She nodded. "As far as my instructions about you are concerned: I received them late last night. After our—now how shall I put it—our...er... romantic encounter? No, I don't think that sounds right, do you?" He paused, smiling lazily at her bowed head, the heavy curtain of her hair being unable to hide the deep flush that surged over her features.

"It would appear," he continued blandly, "that the French government are very anxious that no harm should come to you. Very keen indeed to see that you are rescued with all possible speed. I really have no idea why—have you?"

"I—I haven't the faintest notion." She looked up in surprise. "How extraordinary. And how did they know about...about possible trouble last night?" she asked.

"I have been warning everyone in sight for weeks, that there would be 'trouble' as you put it. Apparently the French and British governments are rather more clued-up than the residents of Ouanda."

"I can understand the French government connection. After all, Ouanda used to be part of their colonial empire, didn't it? And they must have interests to protect, like the diamond mine, I suppose. But—but why the British government?" she asked.

"Because I was here, on the spot, of course," he answered.

"But what's that got to do with anything?"

"It's a long story, Emily, and like the trouble at the mine, best left for another day. I'll just go and get some more logs to build up the fire for the night, and then I think it will be time for you to put your head down and go to sleep."

She couldn't prevent herself from shivering as she thought about the people at the mine. Ludo was someone who obviously didn't mince his words, and if he quite clearly didn't want to talk about what had happened...it must have been terrible. She felt sick as she thought again of the dead African lying stretched out in the road, and—and poor Andrew Sinclair. . . .

Emily watched as Ludo's tall, forceful figure strode off into the small wood. She disliked him intensely, of course, but at the same time . . . . She sighed. However much she might resent the fact, and she certainly did, there was no doubt that she felt . . . well, safe with him. If it hadn't been for his prompt arrival this morning—was it only this morning—she'd have gone out of her mind with terror. Or worse, she could have been killed.

Sitting hunched over the fire, Emily's tired mind tried to grapple with the unwelcome truth: that without Ludo's help she would be dead by now. She owed her entire existence not to her fair-weather friends, nor to her wealth and all that it could buy, but to this extraordinarily hard, tough man who had so casually plucked her from the very jaws of death. And precious little thanks he's had for his action, a small voice whispered inside her head.

She suddenly jumped as a twig snapped and she twisted around, sighing with relief, to find that it was Ludo returning with his arms full of logs. Emily sank down on to the earth again, watching with dazed eyes as Ludo knelt and placed the wood on the fire. His bush shirt was stretched tightly across his broad shoulders, the sleeves rolled up to display his muscular arms. He—he saved my life, she thought bemusedly, flushing as he turned to give her a reassuring smile before continuing to build up the fire for the night.

She owed her life to him, and she would continue to do so. He'd made it very plain that they were in extreme danger. She—she couldn't get out of Ouanda without his help. In fact she was helplessly vulnerable and totally in his power. She had no choice but to depend on him—for everything. She, Emily, who'd never allowed herself to depend on anybody or anything, not since—since the age of fifteen anyway.... Swiftly and adroitly she suppressed the unwanted memories and tried to concentrate on her present predicament.

Emily sighed, putting a tired hand distractedly through her hair. Glancing up at the silent girl, Ludo saw the graze on her forehead.

"You've cut yourself. Why didn't you tell me?"

She flinched at his accusatory tone. "It—it didn't seem important."

"In this climate every cut, graze or wound is important," he said sternly, rising and going over to the Land Rover, returning with a small box of medical supplies.

"Come over here to the fire," he commanded her. "Now stand still while I have a look at it." Grasping her chin firmly with one hand, he tilted her face upwards towards him. She shut her eyes as with surprising gentleness he pushed the hair back off her forehead, and swabbed the cut with antiseptic lotion.

"When did you do this?" he asked quietly.

"When I...er...when I was trying to collect some wood for the fire."

"There, that should be all right now." Emily opened her eyes at his words, peeping through her eyelashes at the dark, handsome face bent so closely over hers. His mouth was set in a tight line, the gleaming grey eyes holding an expression she couldn't fathom. He looked fierce and dangerous as he let go of her chin and she took a deep breath, trying to summon up the courage for what she had to say.

"Ludo...." She put a tentative hand on his arm.

"Yes, Emily, what is it?"

"I...er...I haven't thanked you for—for saving my life. I...."

He shrugged, looking down at her with cynical grey eyes. "I was only acting on instructions. Anyone would have done the same."

She turned away to hide the shaft of pain she felt at

his words. Of course he was only "acting on instructions." He'd made that very clear back at the bungalow. He may have saved her life, but he had only come to her rescue because he had been told to. He didn't like her. In fact he'd made it very plain that he despised her and considered her a confounded nuisance. Why should he prove to be any different to anyone else she'd ever known?

Taking a deep breath and trying to ignore the heavy weight of loneliness and depression which seemed to fill her weary body, she felt him put an arm about her waist.

"Poor old Emily. Come along—time for bed." His voice was surprisingly kind as he led her in the bright moonlight to the Land Rover. She was swaying with tiredness, as she saw him raise one of the bench seats which ran along the side of the vehicle, and lift out a plank of wood, covered in padded foam.

"What's that for?" she asked as he slid it in between two grooves in the sides of the benches, before covering the platform he had just made with sleeping-bags and pillows.

"The benches are rather narrow, and we can't have you falling out of bed in your sleep, can we?" he replied with a grin.

"Aren't—aren't we sleeping in tents? Surely that's what you do when you go camping?"

"If I'm staying anywhere for a length of time, of course I use a tent. But it's far too cumbersome to put it up and take it down every day, which is what we will be doing. Besides, hyenas proliferate in this area, and far from them being the scavengers that most people think they are, they are quite happy to do their own hunting."

"Ugh!" she shuddered, looking around her nervously and then glanced back at the Land Rover. "Are we... are we both... ? I mean, do we... ?"

"Are we sleeping in the back of the Land Rover? Yes we are," he said shortly. "You'll be quite safe, Emily," he added sardonically, looking at her apprehensive face. "Raping you is the last thing I have on my mind at the moment."

"Very funny!" she snapped, irritated to find her cheeks flushing under his amused gaze. "What—what shall I wear?"

"I have no idea," he shrugged. "What did you bring with you?"

"How in the hell do I know—you packed my bag," she said petulantly, shivering with exhaustion.

"Well, you'd better have a look and see." He handed her the case. "You can wash with some of the water in the can, but go easy on it. It's all we have until I find a fresh source."

Ludo lit a Calor gas lantern which she used to search through her case. What a ghastly collection, she thought as she rummaged through her belongings, picking out her sponge bag and a slim nightdress. Going behind a tree to change, she squinted in the moonlight down at her breasts practically exposed in the thin, white silk gown. Heaven knows what he'll think, she said to herself, washing away the grime of the journey with a soft wet flannel. I'm too tired to care, anyway.

As she made her way back to the Land Rover Ludovic raised his eyebrows but apart from his lips, which twitched with amusement, he made no comment. She lifted aside the mosquito net, crawling thankfully into the back of the vehicle to lie on top of her sleeping bag, it being far too hot and humid a night to get inside the wadding itself.

Emily turned over to face the side of the vehicle as she heard Ludo approach and climb inside to join her. "Good night Emily," he said in a quiet voice, "sleep well."

"Yes," she murmured. "I'll try." But however hard

she tried, she was unable to prevent images of the day from crowding into her mind. She saw again Andrew Sinclair's body, and the man who had accompanied him, whose outstretched figure on the road had first alerted her to the danger she was in. She tried clamping her eyes shut, but the pictures of the dreadful massacre refused to go away.

She tossed and turned in the dark, certain that never had she felt so lonely and bereft. There wasn't a person in the whole world who cared whether she lived or died—except the French government it seemed—and that was obviously because of her wealth. What was going to happen to them? Would she and Ludo be killed, as she very much feared the people at the mine had been?

As the moon went behind a cloud, the resulting darkness seemed to press down on her like a heavy weight. She was suddenly swamped by an overwhelming surge of desolation and turned to bury her face in the pillow, frantically trying to muffle her frightened sobs. Ludo would surely despise her more than ever if he heard her being so weak and silly.

"Everything will be all right, Emily. Don't cry. You must try and go to sleep." Ludo's voice was quiet in the darkness.

"I—I have tried, Ludo, really I have," she sniffed. "I—I can't seem to forget what h-h-happened." She couldn't prevent a small sob from escaping as the tears began to flow again.

"Oh Emily!" He sighed softly, reaching over to pull her unhappy figure into his arms. Producing a handkerchief he gently wiped the tears from her eyes, and then settled down on the sleeping-bag with Emily firmly clasped against his warm, hairy chest.

"Now, go to sleep," he said firmly, placing her head against his broad shoulder. "You know I'll beat you black and blue if you don't!"

She gave a small grunt of amusement as she snuggled against his strong, firm body. He was dressed only in a pair of shorts. Surprisingly, considering how much she disliked Ludo, she felt totally safe with the comfort of his arms about her, and within minutes she was fast asleep.

"COME ON YOU BRUTE!" Emily swore at the jack of the Land Rover as she tried to put it in position. She looked again at the instruction booklet. Yes, she was putting it in the right place, so why wouldn't it work? "Damn and blast!" she shouted with rage, trying yet again to do the job that Ludo had insisted she perform. She glanced over at Ludo's tall figure as he leaned against a tree, but apart from an amused grin as he considered the map in his hands, he made no comment.

At last the jack slid into place, and she began to turn the lever to allow her to get at the punctured tyre. "Bloody man!" she swore under her breath. Lounging over there, and making her do all the work. I hope his bacon and eggs choke him to death, she thought viciously, remembering their breakfast together that morning.

She had woken up after her first night in the Land Rover, it taking her some minutes to remember exactly where she was. The sleeping-bag beside her was empty, and she blushed as she remembered her unhappiness in the night and Ludo's comforting arms about her. She looked swiftly down at her nightdress. Yes, she was still decent—just—thank goodness.

She crawled toward the open rear door of the Land Rover, and saw that Ludo had got a fire going and was busily cooking breakfast. He looked up as she stepped down on to the ground, and gave her a smile. "Good morning, Emily. You remind me of Botticelli's Venus arising from the waves."

His warm, friendly smile struck her like a blow, and

she was suddenly breathless. "She—she wasn't wearing any clothes," Emily said in confusion, biting her lip in frustration at being so silly as he roared with laughter.

"Hope springs eternal, Emily!" He smiled, sitting back and regarding her with his head on one side, allowing his eyes to roam over her figure, partially revealed by the thin silk nightdress.

She blushed a deep crimson and scurried for the shelter of the trees. He really is the end—the absolute end, she thought, as she pawed desperately through the clothes in her case a few minutes later. No, not a trace of one, she realised with dismay, and draping herself in a towel she went back to where he was busy cooking.

"Er...Ludo," she said hesitatingly. "Have you... did you...er...pack any more of my things?"

"No," he replied, without turning around. "Only what you've got in that case of yours."

"But—but I don't seem to have any underclothes," she said with annoyance.

"I'm sure I threw in some pairs of pants." He turned to look at the flustered girl.

"Yes—yes you did. But...." Oh what does it matter, she thought. This was clearly neither the time nor the place for the normal delicacies of life.... "But you didn't pack a bra," she explained.

He shrugged. "I'm sorry, Emily. You'll have to wear what you wore yesterday."

"But—but I wasn't wearing one!" she wailed.

"Nor you were," he agreed with a grin. "Never mind. However, if you're desperate, I can always try and help you construct something—I'll measure you now, if you like."

"Oh, go to hell!" she retorted, trying to ignore his laugh as she stalked back into the wood with as much dignity as she could muster.

The argument at breakfast didn't improve matters

between them. She felt on edge, partly because of her anger at his stupidity in not packing a bra, and also because the only clean top she could find was a T-shirt she had forgotten she possessed. Clearly it must have shrunk in the wash. Ludo's whistle of appreciation as she joined him at the fire merely confirmed her fears as to exactly how tight and revealing it was.

"Eat up," he said, handing her a plate of bacon and eggs.

"I never eat breakfast." She shuddered with distaste. "Just coffee please."

Ludo sighed. "I thought we'd had this argument last night," he said in a hard voice. "I find it very boring to have to go through it all again, Emily. I'll repeat myself just once more, and if I have any trouble with you after that, you will indeed be very sorry! As I said, you must eat, even if you don't want to. It is very easy to become run down in this climate, and I don't intend to have the bother of looking after someone who's ill. Okay?"

"I'm sick and tired of you telling me what to do, and—and what not to do," she shouted at him in a sudden fury. "Who in the hell do you think you are?"

"I'm the person who is trying to save your stupid neck—that's who I am!" he retorted angrily, rising from the fire in one fluid motion and grabbing her firmly by the shoulders.

"Now—you either eat up your breakfast, or I'll put you across my knee and spank you like the silly little girl you are!" His face was a mask of grim implacability.

"You—you wouldn't dare!" she snarled, glaring up at him defiantly and trying to ignore the shivers of apprehension running up and down her spine.

"You know I would, Emily. Or maybe," he purred menacingly, putting his hard arms about her, "you'd like me to kiss you again, like I did the other night?"

She gasped as he lowered his dark, handsome head

towards her. "Okay...okay," she cried, hurriedly turning her face away. "I'll eat your damn breakfast— you...you rotten bully!"

Still holding her firmly, he buried a hand in her hair forcing her head back, and tilting her face towards him. "And no more nonsense about eating anything I put before you?" he insisted, his hard angry eyes boring down into hers.

"You're hurting me!" Emily moaned. She felt her head beginning to throb as she inwardly seethed with impotent rage.

"Come on. I want you to promise me to cut out all this stupid nonsense. It's nothing but a waste of time. Promise me." Ludo's tone was silky with menace.

"Yes, I—I promise you," she gasped through clenched teeth.

"That's a good girl," he said with cynical amusement, relaxing the pressure somewhat. "You may not believe me, but by the time we reach civilization, I do believe that you might just—but only just—become a reasonable member of the human race. It will be a nice change from the spoilt brat you are at the moment."

"I really hate you!" she cried, ashamed and humiliated to feel revealing tears of frustration welling up in her eyes.

"Do you Emily?" he asked softly. "Well, it's a nice, positive emotion, isn't it. Anything must be better than going around bored to death, like you have for most of your life."

Her eyes widened. "How did...." She clamped her mouth shut.

"How did I know?" he said, completing the sentence. "Because I knew, very well indeed, someone just like you a long time ago, and because I'm a very wise old man—that's how. Now—" he released her "—go and eat your breakfast."

She had done as she was told, and they had refuelled

and packed up before driving off in silence. The journey that morning had been uneventful, till about noon, when he had suddenly stopped the Land Rover. He had got out to listen for a moment, before jumping in and driving swiftly for the shelter of some trees.

"What's happening?" she asked, Ludo having ordered her to jump out as he whipped a camouflage net from the back and draped it quickly over the vehicle.

"Helicopter," he said briefly, and pushed her roughly under the Land Rover, joining her a moment later.

"I can't hear anything, and there's no need to be so rough!" she grumbled. She suddenly felt a wind as leaves and dust swirled under the vehicle and a thudding noise filled her ears. Grabbing Ludo in fright, she buried her head in his shoulder as the sound of the helicopter's rotor blades seemed to go on and on.

Eventually there was silence and she opened her eyes, looking into his face only inches from her own. "Can—can we get out now?" she asked, flustered by the fact that his hard, firm body was lying half across hers, effectively pinning her to the hard ground.

"Not yet," he said calmly. "We must make sure that it's gone completely away, and not likely to return."

"How—how do you know it was an enemy plane? It might have been looking for us, for—for all you know...." She tried to wriggle out from beneath him, blushing at the gleam of amusement in his eyes as he made no effort to assist her.

"My dear Emily," he murmured, with a sardonic grin on his face. "Despite the fact that I'm enjoying your...er...movements—I do feel you would do well to save your strength. We'll be out of here in a minute."

"Really!" she gasped at the effrontery of the dreadful man. "If you think...."

"I think...I think that you are a delicious armful, Emily." His voice was faintly husky as he continued to grin lazily down at her.

Opening her mouth to give him the withering retort that his audacious remarks deserved, she caught an unusually warm gleam in his eyes. Nervously she flicked her tongue over lips that seemed suddenly dry, closing her eyes in panic as her heart began to pound loudly and she felt a deep flood of crimson sweep over her face.

"Silent, Miss Lambouchere? Now that is a novelty!"

Emily ignored the taunting words, trying desperately to control her breathing which seemed to be behaving oddly.

"Please—please can we get out of here. Surely it's—it's safe enough now..." she pleaded as she felt her body tremble beneath him.

In the silence which followed her words she cautiously opened her eyes, blinking up at him in the half light. The face gazing down at her seemed unusually grim and stern, and without a word he rolled away, banging his head against the Land Rover's chassis as he did so. Serve him right, she thought, pleased at his discomfort as he swore under his breath. And then suddenly she felt ashamed of herself. He had, after all, saved her life yet again—if that really was an enemy helicopter that had just flown over. It was no good, of course, trying to say anything. He obviously didn't want or need her thanks.

Dejectedly, she allowed him to help her out from beneath the Land Rover. She stood brushing the leaves and dust from her body, as he went to the back of the vehicle returning with a thermos.

"I made some coffee this morning at breakfast so we might as well have some now," he announced in a hard voice. Gratefully accepting a cup, she watched as he spread a map out on top of the bonnet of the Land Rover.

"It's far too complicated to explain all the ins and outs of the situation at the moment. However, Emily, you can take it from me that with two mercenary armies at each other's throats, plus General Ngaro's own national guard, it is open season on any vehicle. Especially one such as our long-base Land Rover, which could be mistaken for a small army truck. I hope that disposes of your question about whether that helicopter was friendly or not."

"But surely we're far away enough from the mine now?"

Ludo sighed. "Emily, the whole country has gone up in flames. Can't you understand that? Ouanda is firmly in the grip of a civil war. It's a case of shoot first, and ask questions later!"

There was a pause while she tried to comprehend the enormity of what he was saying. "So—how are we going to get out of the country?" she asked.

"Come over here and look at the map." He bent over the bonnet. She moved over to stand beside him, trying to make some sense of the unfamiliar outlines.

"Here is Ouanda," he said, pointing at what seemed to be a big square in the middle of the map. "Come on, come closer and get a good look at it," he commanded. "Understanding, and clearly following what I say now, may save your life." Feeling strangely reluctant, she allowed him to grasp her waist as she leant beside him over the vehicle.

"Now to the north is Chad," he continued. "Not the most salubrious country. Amnesty International's report on conditions there certainly wouldn't encourage anyone to pay it a visit, however fleeting!" He turned and grinnned at her.

Goodness he's attractive, she thought suddenly, as he turned back to his small drawing. She gazed at his dark head, the hair curling slightly as it met the back of his neck, and the shadow of his long dark eyelashes on his high cheek-bones. His broad shoulders were hunched up, the shirt stretched tightly across his wide back....

"Come on, Emily—concentrate," he said irritably, looking sideways at the woman's slightly glazed eyes and softly parted lips. "Are you all right?"

"Oh yes...yes," she blushed, wondering why her heart was beating so fast.

"Right, that's Chad discarded. The Sudan, to the east, is too far away and the Bahaists and Communists have a running war there anyway. Down here, in the south," he said, pointing with his finger, "are Zaire and Congo Brazzaville—the old Belgian Congo to you and I. Neither is a particularly attractive choice, and to get there we would have to travel through the Congo rain forest. I could do it, but I doubt that you would survive."

"So where can we go?" She suddenly felt frightened. "There doesn't seem to be anywhere left."

"The Cameroon," he pointed, "here, in the west. It won't be a particularly easy journey, I'm afraid. At the moment we are travelling south, to circle around Ouanda's capital Dekoa, and when we've gone far enough we must turn west, towards the Cameroon. We'll have to cross two rivers," he drew marks on the map, "here and here, and then, unless I can avoid it, we will have to go through part of the rain forest, before swinging up north again to the Cameroon border."

"How do you know the Cameroon will be any better than the other countries you've mentioned?" Emily asked. "They all sound dreadful!"

"It has a relatively stable government, and there is considerable French influence and investment there; enough to keep things quiet, anyway. It's my guess that the French will send in some paratroopers to bring order here in Ouanda, before long, but unfortunately, we can't wait."

"Will it take us very long? How far is it?"

"We'll have to travel about two hundred miles in all—but that's very much a guess—it depends what we meet on the way," he answered.

"Oh, that's not too far, then," she said with relief. He shrugged noncommittally, looking at her face only inches from his own.

"Are you all right? You look a bit flushed," he said putting a hand on her forehead and holding her wrist. "Your pulse is rather fast, otherwise you seem okay."

"Of course I am," she retorted breathlessly, colouring slightly under his intense gaze. "it's—it's just that it was a bit claustrophobic under the Land Rover. That's all."

"Come on," he said, folding up the map and stowing it away with the camouflage net before climbing into the driving seat. "Come on, Emily. It's time we were off."

"Come on, come on," she muttered under her breath. I'm fed up to the back teeth with being ordered around, she thought, joining him in the vehicle. I really hate him! She glowered at his profile as he started the engine. The trouble was, she thought reflectively a few minutes later, she wasn't sure—not entirely sure, anyway—that she really did hate him. He seemed to be having a rather peculiar effect on her, and one that was not at all welcome.

"How long is it going to take us to cover the two hundred miles?" she asked, some time later.

"I really don't know, Emily," he replied. "It all depends on what the terrain is like, and what difficulties we encounter. Things like a puncture, for instance, will slow us up." He grinned sideways at her. "'Dear God, please don't let us have a puncture' should feature in your prayers every night, without fail."

Half an hour later, going over a rough piece of ground, the vehicle began to shake. Ludo brought it to a halt, and got out to see what was wrong. He came around to Emily's door, and opened it.

"Emily," he said, shaking his head sorrowfully. "I don't think you can have been a good girl. You certainly haven't been praying hard enough—we have a puncture, I'm afraid!"

She laughed at his lugubrious expression, and jumped down on to the ground. It was the last laugh she was to have for some time, as he swiftly began to unbolt the spare wheel carried on the bonnet of the vehicle.

"Here you are, Emily," he said, rolling the wheel towards her.

"What do you mean?" she demanded apprehensively. "You aren't...? You can't be expecting me to change the wheel?"

"Just take your time, and it won't prove too hard," he replied blandly, fetching the jack and the instruction booklet for her use.

"You must be joking!" she cried angrily. "Me? Change a wheel? I...I've never changed a wheel in my whole life..." she spluttered. "What's wrong with you? You look big enough—and ugly enough—to do it yourself!"

"Such compliments!" he laughed. "Just get on with it, Emily. We haven't all day, you know."

She stood glaring at his face, now stern and impersonal, as her instinctive urge to defy his command ebbed away. She knew well enough that he was capable of doing anything—anything to see that his orders were carried out, and she certainly didn't want another confrontation like this morning....

Emily had shrugged and turned away in silence to do as she was told. Now, as she tightened up the last of the wheel nuts, she looked sorrowfully and petulantly at her broken finger nails. What her manicurist would say when she saw Emily's nails, didn't bear thinking about. And as for her hair...! Poor Leonard would have a fit.

She'd never be able to go into his salon again...never! And it's all that man's fault, she fumed, as she stood back and regarded her handiwork.

"There you are," she shouted, going over and throwing the instruction book at him as hard as she could. "I've done the job for you, you—*you pansy*! Poor little mummy's boy didn't want to get his dainty little hands dirty—did he?" she yelled, trembling with rage. He easily fielded the book and walked towards her with a lazy smile.

"Come and have a wash," Ludo said, ignoring her outburst and taking her arm, led her towards the back of the Land Rover. "You did very well and took far less time than I thought you would." He wrung out a wet flannel and wiped her dirty face and hands.

Slightly mollified by his unexpected praise, she still wasn't prepared to forgive him. "Just look at my hands," she wailed, "and I've broken two nails!"

He sighed, and picked her up, placing her none too gently on the tail-board of the Land Rover. "Emily! Emily!" he said, shaking his head. "Just when I think there's some hope for you, you start behaving stupidly again. Why do you think that I made you change the wheel?"

"I don't know," she shrugged. "Knowing you, it was sheer bloody-mindedness, I expect."

"My dear girl. You obviously don't know me, and I haven't even started to be bloody-minded, as you put it. Neither am I a pansy, which I can prove right here and now, if you like!" The savage, ruthless twist of his lips made her shiver.

"No. No. I...I'm sorry...." Emily blushed, squirming with confusion and unable to escape as he stood facing her, arms outstretched, his hands placed on either side of her.

"Very well," Ludo regarded her sternly. "It seems as if yet another lesson is called for. Firstly, life is all about surviving, Emily. Keep that firmly in the front of your mind. In order for us to survive, you must obey my orders immediately, instantly, and at the double. Because if you don't, if you hesitate or try to argue every decision with me, you and I are likely to end up very dead indeed. Are you hearing me loud and clear?" he demanded, gazing firmly into her large, blue eyes.

Emily nodded silently, as he continued. "You may, if you wish, regard the next few days as an intensive period of 'square bashing.' In order to get your instant obedience, I intend to be hard, ruthless and totally un-reasonable—all the things you have been swearing about, in fact. Now, you can make it easy or hard on yourself; the decision is up to you. Do you under-stand?"

"Yes," she whispered, looking down at her clenched fingers.

"I didn't ask you to change that wheel for a laugh," he said in a warmer tone of voice. "If anything hap-pened to me, you must be able to keep going. Surely you can see that?" He squatted down in front of her, taking her hands in his.

"What do you mean—'if anything happens to you'" and she looked at him in fright.

"Exactly what I said. Either one of us could get shot, or have an accident. This isn't a day out at Ascot you know. I don't want to frighten you unnecessarily, but it's only fair to tell you that we will be very lucky to survive the journey. A lot of things can go wrong, and probably will. Now, I've been trained to survive in the wild. You haven't, and I'm trying to make you as self-sufficient as possible, as fast as I can. Later on we'll have some practice with a gun...."

"Oh, I can shoot, all right," she assured him eagerly.

"Really?" He looked sceptical.

She gave him a small, rueful smile. "Ludo...will you promise not to be angry if—if I remind you of my past? You know—grouse moors in August, the Scottish Highlands in September... ?''

"My dear Emily—if you can shoot straight, I'll forgive you anything!" he laughed and pulled her to her feet.

"We are going to survive, aren't we? I mean, nothing is going to happen to you, is it?" she asked anxiously, her hands still in his.

"I'm not turning my toes up yet, if that's what you mean!" he smiled ruefully down at her. "I've trained a lot of men in my time, Emily, and so you can take my word for it that I know a born survivor when I see one. They aren't necessarily the nicest of people; their ruthless self-interest tends to get in the way of any humanitarian feelings. So, I don't know whether you will be pleased or sorry, if I tell you that you are much tougher, and far more ruthless, than you have any idea of at present.''

Ludo ran a finger down her soft cheek. "Oh yes, Emily, you'll survive all right—with or without me.''

"I...I...." His touch on her skin made her tremble, and she gazed at him in confusion for a moment. There was an expression in his eyes that she couldn't fathom, as he swiftly bent to brush his mouth over her lips.

"Right," he said a moment later. "Jump in, Emily. We've spent quite enough time here. We must be off, and quickly!"

Despite his urge to hasten, she walked slowly to her side of the vehicle, her eyes clouded with bewilderment. She didn't like him; she didn't like him at all, did she? So why—why was she disappointed that his kiss had been so brief? She looked at his profile in bafflement as they recommenced their journey.

CHAPTER FOUR

IT WAS MID-AFTERNOON before Ludo stopped the Land Rover in a small grove of trees, looking intently at the apparently deserted farmstead in front of them. There had been little conversation during the day, other than his request for occasional directions. Ludo had decided that she should be able to read a map, and she had been guiding them as best as she could, mostly across what he called the savannah grasslands. The countryside had begun to change after a while, their progress slowing down as they made their way through a more wooded terrain.

"I want you to stay here," he said, reaching behind him and unclipping a long slim cupboard fixed to the roof of the vehicle. He removed two rifles, one of which he passed to her. "It kicks to the left," he said, "so adjust accordingly if necessary." He jumped down and ran crouched towards the farmhouse, before disappearing behind it.

The wait seemed interminable as she broke open the gun, slotted in the cartridges and practiced sighting the rifle through his open window. Suddenly there was a movement, and—and it wasn't Ludo! The figure seemed to be wearing a white coat of some description, as he or she moved along behind a small wall. Emily had a moment of indecision, and then raising the gun, waited for the person's next move. Remembering Ludo's advice, she mentally adjusted to allow for the rifle's miss-sight, and rapidly fired twice as the figure moved.

She waited shaking, for a couple of moments, but as nothing seemed to happen she rearmed the rifle and got down cautiously, walking slowly over to the wall. Ludo must have heard the shot—why hadn't he appeared? She began to feel sick with apprehension.

"Well done, Emily. Really excellent shooting!" Ludo smiled as he got up from behind the wall, removing the white coat he had put on.

"You crazy man!" she gasped, sagging with relief. "I—I could have killed you. What in the hell do you think you're playing at?" she yelled, anger quickly taking over from fear. "I could put a hole through you right this minute—and serve you right if I did!" She shook with tension.

"Now, now," he said soothingly, taking the gun from her trembling hands and putting an arm around her shoulder as he led her towards the house. "I had to know if you were capable of shooting someone in cold blood, and I also had to find out just how good a shot you were. You passed both tests with flying colours. I said you were a born survivor, didn't I?"

"I didn't do so well. I—I should have shot you dead! And I wished I had, while I was at it," she added viciously.

"Oh Emily—what a splendid girl you are!" he laughed. "I don't see why you should be so angry with me. I did, after all, believe you when you said you were a good shot. That's why I said the rifle kicked to the left, when it actually kicks to the right."

"Very funny!" she hissed, deliberately treading hard on his foot as he stood aside to let her enter the house.

"Sorry," he said with a grin, looking down at his boots. "Steel toe caps!"

She glared at him, and then leant against a wall laughing weakly as the tension of the last few minutes drained away. "You'd better be careful in future, Ludo, because I'll remember what you said about the rifle."

"You are a very good shot, Emily. I promise to tread very, very carefully in future," he smilingly assured her. "Now, you will be pleased to hear that there is a rusty and antiquated shower outside the kitchen. The inhabitants seemed to have left in a hurry, which isn't too reassuring. However, I think we'll take a chance, and freshen up quickly. You go and have a shower, while I bring the Land Rover around to the back of the house."

"Don't forget a towel and some soap," she said as he turned to leave. "I'll need a change of clothing too," she added. "I've got nothing left to wear. Can I borrow something of yours?"

"I'll have a look and see what I've got," he said, leaving to move their vehicle.

The water was rusty from having been in the tank for some time, but gloriously hot, thanks to the sun's rays beating down on the thin metal tank. It was, Emily told herself, definitely and absolutely the most wonderful shower she had ever had in her whole life. To feel clean again, after—how long was it—only two days. Somehow, the party at the mine seemed light years away.

She quickly dried herself on one of Ludo's dark green towels which she had appropriated for herself and put on the bush shirt he had provided. Even though she was five foot ten, the shirt was far too long for her. So what, she thought, it was better than nothing, wasn't it? She rolled the sleeves up, and then turned to the pair of shorts Ludo had given her. Thank goodness no one she knew was ever going to see her like this—Groucho Marx to the life, she thought with a rueful grin.

Going back into the main room of the house, she decided to ignore Ludo's laughing comment: "Now that's what I call haute couture!"

"When you've finished your joke," she told him coolly, "I want you to fetch me one of your ties—if you've got such a thing. And if you have a pair of scissors and a needle and cotton, I'd be grateful.''

"Whatever for?'' he asked, with a raised eyebrow.

Emily sighed. "You may have trained many men, Ludo, but you clearly know nothing about women. If I don't look reasonable, I can assure you I won't be reasonable—and you do want me to be reasonable, don't you?'' she said patiently, as if to a child.

"I'll obey your every order, *Herr Commandant*, but in the meantime, will you please let this poor humble soldier have a tie, scissors, a needle and cotton?'' As Ludo continued to stand looking thoughtfully at her, she said sternly, "I want them—now. Come along— chop, chop!''

"Well, well,'' he said slowly. "If that's what a shower does for you, I hate to think what happens when you have a bath!'' With a gesture of surrender he smiled and left the room.

Ludo returned from his shower, towelling his dark hair, to find Emily finished threading his tie through the loops on the waistband of the shorts she was wearing. "There,'' she said with satisfaction, "that's better.''

"It certainly is,'' he agreed, surveying the woman in front of him with evident pleasure. "I can see that I've just lost a good pair of shorts. What have you done to them?''

"I've...er...I've just cut off large chunks from the sides,'' she said airily, "and from the inside of the leg as well. In fact,'' she smiled at him through lowered lashes, "I did cut off most of the leg as well, I must confess, and then I just sort of sewed up what was left....''

"There wasn't much left,'' he agreed with a smile. "Emily Lambouchere—Queen of the Needle!'' he teased, but she just stuck out her tongue at him and walked around the room. "What are you looking for?'' Ludo asked.

"A mirror—idiot!" she said laughing, still feeling in high spirits from her shower.

"There's no need to worry. You look fine," he assured her.

"Ah!" was Emily's only reply, as she hauled a dusty mirror from behind a chair. Propping it up on a table, she stepped back. "Oh no!" she wailed, "just look at my hair!"

"What's the trouble now?"

"It's my hair—it's going curly! It must be the heat and the humidity. Oh, what shall I do?" she moaned.

"Women!" he groaned. "The good Lord preserve me from their vagaries. We must leave, Emily, so stop worrying about your hair, for heaven's sake! I think you look very pretty."

"Pretty? Who wants to look pretty? I used to look smart and attractive—that's what's important. Pretty? Yuck!"

"Tough!" he said brusquely, taking her arm. "We must leave immediately. We've been pushing our luck almost too far as it is. Now," he said, opening the driver's door, "up you get. You will be driving for the rest of the day. And before you say anything, it is to make sure you are familiar with the Land Rover, and not because I'm feeling in a pansy mood!"

"That's not fair..." she flushed, climbing up on to the seat and looking doubtfully at the various dials on the dashboard.

He only laughed in reply, and then proceeded to explain the different features of the eight gears. "Do you think you've got it now?" he asked.

"We'll soon find out, won't we?" she answered grimly, nervously switching on the engine.

Ludo sat watching her tensely for the first ten minutes, and then relaxed against his seat. "You're doing very well. I'll make a man of you yet, Emily!"

"Male chauvinist pig!" she hissed through gritted

teeth, as she wound the heavy vehicle through the trees. "I'm a woman—just in case you hadn't noticed!"

"Oh I have, Emily—indeed I have!" he declared, laughing. "I'm very observant. I've even noticed that you seem to have cut my shirt to bits as well. It fits you like a glove. Very nice—very nice indeed!" he said, laughing again as he noticed the deep tide of crimson which covered her face. "Concentrate on the driving, Emily," he ordered, grinning as she glanced furiously at him, "while I enjoy the scenery inside, as well as out!"

You're stupid, she told herself angrily. You left yourself wide open there. You'd better just get on with the job of trying to drive this huge vehicle, and ignore that dreadful man beside you. It was good advice she gave herself, but easier to say than to do. She was finding his presence increasingly disturbing, and knowing his eyes were on her the whole time, confirmed by a quick sideways glance, made her nervous and ill at ease. Eventually, she settled down as the Land Rover ground over the miles, the going becoming easier as they found a track through the forest.

"Okay this will do. Stop here," he said some hours later, as they left the forest and faced a wide plain. "Just back up here, under the trees. Fine." He got out and came around to help her out. Her legs were stiff and her arms ached from wrestling with the heavy wheel.

"You've done very well," he assured her. "In fact—although I don't want you to get a swelled head—I'm very proud of your progress."

Emily flushed with pleasure at his praise, and stretched with relief. "I know what you're going to say next, Ludo, so you can save your breath. Little Red Riding Hood is going off to fetch the firewood, right now!"

"Are you casting me in the role of the wolf?" His hazy eyes gleamed with amusement.

"If the cap fits...." She grinned over her shoulder as she walked in amongst the trees. There seemed to be a more plentiful supply than last night, and her arms were almost full when she felt someone touch her back. "Cut it out, Ludo," she said laughingly, as a hand ran up and down her back. She turned, smiling, and then screamed in terror. An enormously long thick arm, with two holes instead of a hand, was investigating her hair.

Abandoning her pile of wood, she ran yelling towards the Land Rover. Her first scream must have alerted Ludo, because she met him half-way, running straight into his arms.

"What's wrong?" he demanded urgently.

"There's a 'thing' in the wood," she gasped, clinging on to him for dear life. "This long arm...and no hand...!" she explained shuddering, burying her head in his broad shoulder.

Cautiously, still clinging tightly to Ludo, she lifted her head and peeped behind her. A large elephant stood regarding them as it swung its trunk slowly back and forth. "It's only curious," Ludo said quietly. "They can be dangerous but it looks as if it's only out for an evening stroll. Just stand still and it will soon go away."

She held her breath as she looked at the magnificent animal. Eventually the elephant grew bored, and turning clumsily, ambled off back into the trees. Emily sighed with relief, turning her head to look up at Ludo. There was a disturbing gleam in his eyes, and she suddenly realised that her arms were still clasped tightly about his neck, her body pressed firmly against his.

"I...I must go and...and get some more wood," she murmured huskily, not able to take her eyes away from his handsome face.

Ludo's arms tightened about her slim figure as he gazed silently down at the woman in his arms, her softly parted lips and the wide blue eyes beginning to cloud with desire.

Emily could feel the warmth of his body through his bush shirt. A deep ache suddenly gripped her stomach, her heart began to pound and her legs felt weak and shaky. She couldn't speak as she felt her body beginning to tremble involuntarily, her cheeks flushing under his disturbing gaze.

Her trembling awoke a response in him. He gave a muffled groan and crushed her tightly against his hard, firm chest, his mouth claiming hers in an invasive, fierce and possessive kiss.

Instinctively she tried to protest, her hands fluttering helplessly as he held her so firmly and implacably against him. His mouth which had been so forceful, gradually became softer and warmer, and she found herself responding to the insistent probing of his lips and tongue. Emily found her lips parting under his, scarcely aware of her response as her body was filled with a trembling excitement, a liquid fire of desire coursing through her veins.

Suddenly, too suddenly, it was over. Ludo withdrew his mouth and looked down at her lovely face in the gathering dusk. Swearing briefly under his breath, he let her go abruptly, turning without a word to stride back to the Land Rover. Emily's dazed eyes followed his figure in consternation, before she too turned away, to slowly gather up the firewood she had dropped.

It wasn't possible, she told herself fiercely. It just wasn't possible! She couldn't be falling in love with Ludo? She couldn't be...could she? She didn't like him, and he certainly didn't like her; the whole thing was absurd. Emily leaned weakly against a tree, suddenly and violently assailed by an overwhelming desire to feel his arms about her once again, the warmth of his body next to hers, his mouth on her lips....

She tried valiantly to control her wayward mind, but

try as she might, she could not banish her speculative and feverish thoughts of how it would be if Ludo made love to her. He must be very experienced, she realised, while she ... she'd never cared enough about any of her boyfriends, certainly not enough to do more than let them kiss her good-night. But now ... ? Now, she felt overwhelmingly excited and sick at one and the same time. She realised, with mounting confusion, that their embrace just now had awakened feelings she hadn't known before. Blushing furiously in the gathering darkness of the small wood, she realised that she wanted him to make love to her, more than she had wanted anything in her whole life.

Dinner had been a silent meal. They had both, she noted, avoided looking directly at one another and were very careful not to touch each other, even accidentally.

"I—I think I'll turn in now, if that's all right?" she said, stacking away their plates. "I'm ... very tired. It's been a long day."

"Fine," he said shortly. "I'll just sit out here and have a cigar. Good night Emily."

"Er ... good night," she replied, going to fetch her case. She'd taken the opportunity to wash her things at the homestead, and now she hung them on some branches before going into the wood to change for the night. She realised, with a sinking heart, that she had just washed her only nightdress. The thought of sleeping in the shirt and shorts she had worn during the day was more than she could bear. Draping a thin cotton towel around herself she went back to the vehicle, moving silently past Ludo who sat quietly smoking with his back to her, and climbed into the bed he had made ready while she changed.

Emily tossed and turned in the hot, humid night. She ached all over and it wasn't just from the weariness of the day's travel. Her body trembled with an urgent longing for Ludo's touch, her mouth for the touch of his warm lips. She didn't know if she was falling in love with him, or if it was just lust that she felt. She wished, desperately, that she had had some previous experience to guide her. She clenched her teeth and rolled herself into a ball as she fought her feelings, desperately trying to find relief in sleep.

He'd made it plain that he despised her and everything she stood for. Her feelings couldn't and wouldn't be reciprocated, so she must stifle them as firmly as she could. However, it was a long time before she managed to find oblivion in sleep.

The next thing she knew was that Ludo was shaking her shoulders, and speaking firmly to her.

"Wha...what is it?" she moaned, still half asleep.

"You've been having a nightmare, Emily," he said. "You were crying bitterly and calling for your mother, I think."

"Oh no!" she groaned. "I haven't done that for ages. I'm sorry Ludo. I—I must have woken you up. That's one of the reasons why I normally take sleeping pills," she told him, running a tired hand distractedly through her hair.

"I'll get you a drink of water," he said, climbing out of the Land Rover and returning with a cup.

The moon became obscured by a cloud, and it was suddenly very dark inside the Land Rover. "I—I can't see very well," she murmured, as she sat up and put out her arms blindly in the direction of the door.

"Here," he said, sliding a comforting arm about her waist and placing the cup in her hand. She gasped nervously as she realised that her towel must have become dislodged during the night, and that she was now lying quite naked in his arms.

"I—I'm sorry to have woken you up," she murmured, flickers of excitement coursing through her body as his arms tightened about her. She leaned against his firm, hard chest savouring the musky masculine scent of his skin.

"Drink up." Ludo's voice sounded hoarse and oddly constrained in the darkness. She could feel his heart beating as rapidly as her own, the warmth of his skin and the strength of his arms about her inducing a feeling of languorous desire.

"Are ... are you still issuing commands—even at this time of the night?" Emily's low laugh was soft and husky, her body trembling as his hand began to gently stroke her slim waist.

"Definitely," he said thickly, his fingers moving slowly up to caress her full breasts. She shivered violently as he touched their rosy tips, already swollen with desire, and with a moan she abandoned the cup, sliding her arms about his neck and pressing herself to his warm, hairy chest.

"Emily!" he groaned, his hands moving over the softness of her skin as he buried his head in the curve of her throat. He ran his lips up her slim neck and across her cheek before his mouth took possession of hers. His kiss was a revelation. His mouth moving over her soft, trembling lips was a delight in its tenderness and warmth. Never could she have believed that such a hard, stern man could be so gentle and tender. And overcome by feelings she hadn't known existed, her fingers buried themselves convulsively in his hair as she moved her body innocently and sensuously against him.

Ludo's frame shook in response to her erotic movements, his kiss deepening as he parted her lips and plundered the softness within.

It was if she was drowning ... Emily thought. Drowning in ecstasy! She felt herself sinking back onto the floor, Ludo's weight crushing her swollen breasts, the scorching heat of his kiss driving all coherent thoughts from her mind.

He removed his mouth to gently and caressingly kiss her eyelids and her brow. Emily gasped as his hands moved over her soft, warm body. No one had ever touched her like that before; she had never imagined that a touch could be so sensual and erotic, so arousing in its devastating effect. She moaned helplessly as she responded ardently to his experienced lovemaking, shaken by great waves of overwhelming desire and totally in the grip of a force beyond her control.

His mouth and hands raised her to unknown heights of shimmering excitement as his lips found hers again, and she felt the increasing strength of his passion as his touch became more urgent, more demanding.

Shocking in its suddenness, the moon came out from behind the clouds. Flooding in through the windows of the vehicle, it bathed their bodies in a shaft of silver light. Startled, Emily opened her eyes. Suddenly feeling inexplicably frightened, she made a tortured sound of protest as she tried to drag her lips away from his. "Please," she gasped. "Oh, please, Ludo...."

He froze, propping himself up on his arms and looking down at her in the moonlight. "What is it, Emily?" he demanded roughly, his voice sounding harsh and breathless. "Have you just been teasing me—leading me on...?"

"No!" she cried desperately. "I...It's just that... I've never—never made love with anyone before. I...."

"What! Oh my...!" he groaned, his body shaking with tension.

"I'm sorry...I didn't mean to be stupid..." she whispered tearfully. "I just—just felt frightened for a moment. Please Ludo..." she begged, as he slowly withdrew from her arms. "I wasn't teasing you, truly I wasn't."

Moving slowly as if drugged, he sat up beside her, his face deeply etched with pain as he ran trembling hands through his hair. "I shouldn't have...heaven knows I didn't intend for things to..." he broke off, his voice husky and tortured with self-disgust.

"Oh please...." Emily knelt up beside him, placing her soft arms about his shoulders. "I do want you to—to make love to me Ludo," she murmured. "I—I don't know what came over me. I'm sorry to be so silly and inexperienced...."

"For heaven's sake Emily! Never apologise for innocence..." he groaned in despair, gently removing her hands from his shoulders and wrapping the discarded towel about her body, ignoring her wounded, tearful eyes.

"Oh Ludo..." she whispered in distress, not clearly understanding what had happened, her whole body still on fire from his lovemaking. She put a hand to his cheek, gasping with shock as he flinched from her touch.

"Don't—don't you understand? Can't you see that I'm supposed to be looking after you, guarding you...?" He ground out the words through clenched teeth. "Please, don't make things more difficult for me, Emily!"

"I wasn't teasing you," she pleaded, unable to prevent the tears, the hopeless, aching tears from running down her cheeks. How could he have raised her to such—such overwhelming ecstasy and then rejected her? Didn't he understand...? Couldn't he see what he was doing to her...? A deep throbbing pain seemed to grip the pit of her stomach, and she writhed in torment. "I—I wasn't teasing you..." she repeated tearfully.

"I know you weren't, Emily," he said heavily. "I shouldn't have got carried away—it's all my fault." He turned away and lay on his back, staring at the roof of the Land Rover. "I apologise," he said with a deep sigh as she sobbed quietly in the darkness beside him. "I've behaved very badly, especially to someone who's in my care and under my protection. It—it won't happen again."

"Oh Ludo...please..." she breathed in distress.

"It's all right, Emily. Just go to sleep now—Okay?" He rolled over, lying as far away from her as possible, and lay still.

She lay awake most of the night, as she suspected Ludo did too. Both of them tossed and turned in the darkness, but she didn't dare to touch him, although all her senses were screaming for him. Waves of longing and sexual hunger swept her body, and it was only with the first faint light of the African dawn, that she managed to fall asleep at last.

THE NEXT TWO DAYS were a nightmare. Hardly speaking to each other, they travelled south-west, climbing all the time. The going became rougher, and many times Emily had to jump out of the Land Rover to crowbar large boulders out of the way. Ludo was withdrawn and icily polite, but she made sure that she gave him no cause for complaint, carrying out his commands as swiftly and carefully as she could.

After that disastrous night, Ludo had slept outside the Land Rover on the hard ground, and she hadn't dared to mention the possible presence of hyenas.

Mid-morning on the third day, they had stopped the vehicle and were having a cup of coffee, when they heard the roar of planes overhead. In the distance they saw great billowing clouds of smoke and licking flames. There were the muffled explosions of air-to-ground rockets, and then several planes made low diving runs, spewing out great sheets of flame.

"Napalm," Ludo said briefly. "Whoever's on the ground over there doesn't stand a chance—not a prayer." During the rest of the day they heard explosions of mortar and rockets, coming nearer all the time, and that night Ludo announced that they would have to change their planned route.

"We're going to run into the mercenaries, if we're not careful," he explained, talking reasonably to her for what seemed the first time in days. "We're going to have to go farther south and cross the river here," he pointed to the map. "It will mean going through part of the rain forest, I'm afraid, but I don't see how we can avoid it."

"You—you mentioned napalm earlier today, Ludo. What is it?" she asked quietly.

"It's dreadful stuff. An oil-based incendiary device that burns up the forests, and sticks to people, burning them alive. It's been outlawed by all civilized countries, ever since they saw what happened when the Americans used it in Vietnam."

He paused and looked at her, with the first friendly, if faint smile she'd had from him for a long time. "I like to think I'm pretty tough, Emily, but I've seen its effects, and they're ... well they're just awful," he said grimly. "When I found that cache at Goose Green, I just couldn't believe it. I ..." He closed his mouth with a snap, and busied himself putting more logs on the fire.

"Goose Green?" she said in puzzlement. "But that's ... surely that's in the Falklands? I thought you were supposed to be a professor of zoology. Although I can see that you've been doing nothing but talk in army terms. What are you Ludo—really?"

He shrugged and grinned reluctantly at her. "I am a professor of zoology—attached to London University." He got up and went over to the Land Rover, returning with a book which he handed to her.

The Social Behaviour of the Gorilla she read on the cover, and below, *by Dr. Ludovic Vandenberg*. Opening the book, she looked inside the dust cover at the back, and read that Dr. Ludovic Vandenberg had been born in South Africa, educated in Cape Town and the University of Cambridge.

Following some years in the British army, Dr. Vandenberg resumed his studies, and has led many expeditions to the Congo and Ouandan rain forests to study gorillas. He is famous for his very successful series of television films on primates in general, as well as being Britain's leading authority on the life and habitat of the gorilla.

"Okay," she said slowly, "as curriculum vitae's go, it's very impressive. But how come you were in the Falklands, many years after you left the army, and I still don't understand why you were asked by the French government to look after me. I know you've been using a radio transmitter," she added bitterly. "This 'silly little rich girl' has actually got a pair of eyes in her head—however dim you might think I am!"

"Oh Emily," he said, coming over to sit beside her, taking her hands in his. "I'm...er...truly sorry that I ever said anything so unkind. I—I..." he ran a hand through his hair. "Please forgive me, and put my words down to the extreme...er...anger and frustration of the moment. I was worried about the country going up in flames, and—well, I really don't know what came over me." He paused and coloured slightly. "While I'm at it, I...er...I know I behaved abominably the other night—taking advantage of your innocence. I'm—I'm very sorry for everything that happened."

"It's—it's all right, Ludo," she said breathlessly, looking down at her hands and hoping her hair would hide the tide of crimson she could feel spreading over her face. "Let's just say that we both...er...got carried away, and leave it at that. However, I'm not going to let you off the hook!" she added hurriedly. "You still haven't explained how you can be a professor and in the army, both at the same time."

"Well...er...I was in the army, and I occasionally get called up—that's all."

"Oh yeah," she said vulgarly, "tell that to the marines!" There was a pause, and then she laughed. "You were a marine!" she exclaimed.

"No—not quite. A rather more select bunch, that still call me up from time to time."

"Not the Special Air Service, the SAS?" she asked, her eyes wide with surprise.

"Look, Emily," he said sternly. "I'm not going to confirm or deny anything, so you can keep on guessing until kingdom come. Just take it that I still do get called up occasionally, as I did with your little problem. Incidentally, I'm as intrigued as you are, as to why the French government want you out of Ouanda so badly. Haven't you been able to work it out yet?"

"No, I haven't. It's been puzzling me too."

He spoke briskly. "Right, let's regard this as an intelligence exercise and begin at the beginning. First things first—do you own the Lambouchere Company outright?"

"No. Until I'm twenty-one my trustees run it, and then they continue to have a considerable say in what goes on. Unless I die without leaving any children, and then the trust is dissolved and the company passes free of all encumbrances to a very distant cousin. Why—that's it!" she smiled. "How silly of me not to have thought of it before now. No wonder the French government want to keep me alive!"

"Come on—explain!"

"Well, all my father's family in France were wiped out during the last war," she explained, "and there's only myself and a distant cousin. He's a bit older than me, and very odd—a bearded weirdie in fact. He belongs to some obscure sect that believes that all capitalism is wrong, and that communism is the answer to everyone's prayer. They seem, the sect I mean, to have got religion and communism mixed up; anyway the

Russians don't seem to mind. If I died, he would get control of the company, and hand it on a plate to Russia. Russia then gets a big slice of Ouanda and...."

"And the French government and their investors in Ouanda and neighbouring states wouldn't like that!" he said, completing the sentence.

"Exactly!" she agreed. "You know—I think you should start being practical Ludo," she drawled. "Why don't you hold me for ransom while you're at it? If they want me that badly, maybe you could become a 'silly little rich girl' like me?"

"Don't push your luck, Emily!" he retorted grimly. "I've apologised—both for that and what happened the other night—so let's keep off that dangerous subject, shall we?"

She nodded silently, her face flushing as she remembered their passionate lovemaking.

"Okay, that's one question answered," he said smoothly. "Let's have some more coffee." As he made a fresh jug, Emily looked at him with new eyes. What an extraordinary combination, she thought. A professor who was also a member of the SAS or whatever it was called nowadays. No wonder Bob, back at the mine, had said there was something odd about Ludo. Much of what he had just said, explained the inconsistencies in his behaviour, which had been troubling her.

The thought of Bob and the mine, prompted the next question. "I—I haven't asked you before, Ludo," she said slowly and hesitantly, "mainly because I—I couldn't face the thought of what you'd say. Was—was everyone...was everyone killed at the mine that morning?"

He looked intently at her for a moment and then sighed deeply. "Yes, I'm afraid so. I arrived too late to prevent the massacre. The mercenary troops—Lord knows which bunch of cutthroats they belonged to—they were swarming all over the place. There was nothing I could do, I'm afraid. I managed to put a couple of the workers out of their misery; there was nothing more I could do to save them. Nothing at all.''

"Oh Ludo!" she gazed at him ashen faced. "Even Bob, and poor Amy?''

"I didn't see Bob, so he may have escaped. I hope so.'' He paused. "I'm sorry about Amy, Emily. There was nothing I could do. I—I arrived too late.''

Her eyes filled with tears, as he continued. "I saw Andrew and a worker run to a Jeep and saw that they managed to get away. I hoped they would make it, but I had my doubts when I saw the leader of the mercenaries had a transmitter strapped to his back. He must have called up the aeroplane that strafed the bungalow and Andrew's jeep.''

"Oh, no!" she moaned. "It's so awful...just awful....''

"Now, Emily," he spoke firmly. "I told you life was all about surviving, didn't I? It may sound hard and unfeeling, but there is no point in grieving over what has happened and cannot be mended. Your duty is to the living—first of all yourself, and then me—while I'm in your company that is. If you feel like faltering, just remember your batty cousin—there's no reason why he should benefit from your early death, is there?''

"No." She gave him a rather wobbly and timorous smile. "I...I'll try and remember what you've said.''

"Good girl. Now it's time for bed.''

"Er...Ludo. You don't have to—to sleep on the hard ground, I...I'm worried about the hyenas. I.... er...I promise not to...er....''

"Darling Emily. As a professor of zoology, I must tell you that we left the natural habitat of hyenas some time ago. As an ordinary and very frail man, I must further tell you that I find the prospect of sharing your bed, albeit at the distance of a foot or two, far too tempting a prospect to be entertained. In other words, thank you—but no thank you! We will both be much safer if I continue to sleep outside. So off you go, and I'll see you in the morning."

Emily tossed and turned during the night, unable to sleep for a long time. She knew that she was falling—had fallen—in love with Ludo. For the first time in her life, she had come to rely and depend on someone—totally and utterly. She knew that she could place her absolute trust in Ludo and his ability to look after and defend her. Not just here in the dangerous circumstances in which they found themselves, but for the rest of their lives.

She desperately wanted and needed to express her love, and she wanted and needed him to make love to her. Emily had never made love to anyone in her life, mainly because she had never met a man she even cared sufficiently about to want to give herself freely. She was far too fastidious a person to abuse her body as so many of her promiscuous friends had done.

But now she had met her fate. Maybe without her vast wealth and the stupid, vacuous, unthinking life she had led, Ludo could come to feel for her what she felt for him. But there seemed nothing she could do, here and now, to prove to him that his caring love was of far more importance to her than any money or possessions. She was caught in a vicious circle from which there seemed to be no release.

Because, even if Ludo believed that she had never slept with another man, he was so bound up by his code of honour and his disapproval of her world, that there seemed no chance of them consummating their feelings for one another. But while he might disapprove of her, she knew, with all her newly-awakened senses that he wanted to make love to her, every bit as much as she wanted him.

How shall I bear it, was her last despairing thought as she fell asleep at last.

CHAPTER FIVE

EMILY WOKE THE NEXT MORNING feeling depressed and sluggish. She lay looking up at the roof of the Land Rover, but all she saw was Ludo's dark and handsome face. She knew the next part of their journey would be perilous, but she had complete faith in his ability to surmount all the dangers they might meet. He had talked about survival, and he had been right when he had told her to dismiss all thoughts of the terrible massacre at the mine from her brain. For the next few days all her energies must be concentrated on surviving— just keeping alive. There would be time later to mourn those who had died.

She burned with shame as she remembered her boredom and callous indifference to the needs and desires of other people. All her life she had been cocooned in a warm blanket of wealth and security. Never had she known want and deprivation, never had she expressed a desire for something without it being fulfilled immediately. A snap of her fingers had brought heat, light and sustenance. It was only now, when she found herself without the comfortable trappings of civilization, that she appreciated the true values of life.

Ludo had said that by the end of the journey he would turn her into a reasonable member of society; it looked as if he might succeed. Ludo . . . she hugged herself involuntarily, a shaft of pain flowing through her body. A delicious, and at the same time, a fearful pain. Other men had kissed and tried to make love to her, but none of them had produced the effect that Ludo had, just by looking at her, or touching her lightly. She trembled as she remembered his warm erotic touch on her body, the deep passion of his kisses, and moaned softly as she thought of how much she wanted him. She wanted him, as she had never wanted anyone so much in her life before, and the need and desire of his touch was beginning to tear her apart.

And that's the trouble, she thought sadly, as she sat up hugging her knees. For the first and only time in her life, she wanted something that she couldn't possibly have. What she wanted had to be freely given, and was being most forcefully withheld. With a heavy heart, she crawled out of the Land Rover and went to get dressed.

Following their reasonable discussion last night, their journey that morning should have been a more pleasant affair than the preceding two days; but somehow it wasn't. Tentacles of constraint began to weave through the constricted space of the Land Rover, the atmosphere slowly becoming vibrant with tension. Neither of them said more than the commonplace necessities as the air grew thick with strained, unspoken words.

Emily, glancing sideways through her lashes at Ludo, noticed his clenched jaw, a pulse beating in his temple. She was sharply conscious of his leashed strength and his vibrant masculinity, as his muscular arms wrestled with the wheel over the difficult ground.

Ludo suddenly brought the vehicle to a halt and turned to her, his face tense and strained. "The river is down there," he said harshly, pointing through the trees. "I'm going out to find the best place to try and cross it. There should be a ford somewhere near here, if you've been reading the map properly. Which is unlikely!" he added through clenched teeth.

"That's not fair!" she burst out. "You, yourself, said I was doing quite well. Maybe if I'd spent years in the army, I'd be better at it. You're not being fair!" she repeated angrily.

"Fair? Who said anything about life being fair?" he growled. "Don't be more stupid than you can help, Emily!"

"Oh! Go and look for your damned river," she snapped. "And—and I hope you fall in!" she yelled after his departing figure.

Left alone, Emily sighed and sank back in her seat. It was going to be a great day, if the atmosphere of this morning was anything to go by. There was no need for him to snap and shout at her—what had she done to upset him? Nothing, absolutely nothing that she could see. She sighed again, looking around the clearing at the tall trees.

Oh, my, she thought suddenly. That stupid man has gone off and hasn't given me a gun. What would happen if someone came by now? She'd be totally unprotected. Anything could happen! She knelt up in her seat and opened the gun locker, removing a rifle and ammunition. She opened her door and got down, walking over to stand behind a tree at the edge of the clearing. She felt quite proud of herself. If an intruder came by, they would go straight to the Land Rover, and if need be she would be in a position to have a good shot at them before they knew what was happening. She stood waiting quietly, listening to the birds singing in the trees.

Presently the birds' song stopped and a small furry animal ran quickly past her feet. Someone was coming. She waited breathlessly, and then saw that it was Ludo, approaching from a different direction than the one he had taken on leaving the vehicle. She stood watching him silently as he approached the Land Rover, and was astounded at his violent reaction on discovering that she wasn't inside.

Spinning on one foot, he turned and dived inside, somehow collecting his rifle as he rolled out of the back a second later. Kneeling crouched by the rear of the vehicle, he looked fiercely about him.

"It's all right, Ludo. I'm over here," she called as she walked out from the trees. "I thought I'd...." She got no farther as he raced towards her, grabbing and shaking her shoulders with such force that she dropped the rifle and her teeth rattled in her head.

"What in the hell do you think you're playing at! I told you to stay in the Land Rover," he roared with anger. "Are you completely incapable of understanding anything I say?"

"I—I was being very sensible," she shouted back. "I thought it all out. If someone had come by, I was ready and prepared to defend the Land Rover and myself. It's you that's stupid!" she yelled in his face. "You left me undefended, you—you stupid man!"

"Undefended? You? Hah!" he laughed grimly. "Emily—you'd make a piranha look like a cuddly toy!" He stepped back and looked at her with blazingly angry eyes, lines of strain etched deeply into his face. "An empty-headed, selfish, flibbertigibbet socialite, who never thinks about anything else but herself...." He got no farther. Beyond herself with anger and rage, Emily lashed out and struck him with all her force.

It was a hard, stinging blow across his face, and she got immense satisfaction from its delivery. All her pent-up emotions were released, but as she raised her arm to hit him a second time, her hand never reached its target. He easily and contemptuously caught her wrist, holding it in a vicelike grip, before swiftly bending her arm behind her back and twisting it upwards with cruel force.

"The change I thought I'd discerned in Miss Emily Lambouchere didn't last long, did it?" he hissed quietly and with terrifying menace behind her. "You are still the nasty, spoilt child you were the first evening we met—aren't you?'' he rasped, jerking her hand higher and causing her to gasp with pain. "Aren't you?" he repeated.

Emily gritted her teeth as her eyes filled with tears. She'd never hated anyone as much as she hated him. Never! How could she have thought that she loved him—the swine! "I'm waiting for your answer, Emily,'' he purred ferociously in her ear.

"You can...you can wait...forever!" she gasped, the pain shooting up her shoulder, numbing the muscle in her arm. "I—I don't care—I don't care what you do to me," she panted, almost fainting with the pain. 'I—I have changed...and if you don't—don't see that... nothing's going to matter ever again.'' She slumped to the ground sobbing helplessly.

Ludo sighed deeply before squatting down and putting his arms about the weeping woman. Silently he began to massage her arm and shoulder, carefully and tenderly. Presently he put his arm around her tearful figure and led her slowly back to the Land Rover, lifting her gently into her seat. Still silent, he resumed his place and drove them down to the river's bank.

Emily felt numb, paralysed by what had happened, devoid of all thought and emotion. The events of the last few minutes had left her bereft of any feelings, just a great unhappy ache inside her body. She sat slumped in her seat, staring sightlessly in front of her.

They forded the river with ease, and some miles on Ludo halted the Land Rover. As he cut the engine, she heard a roaring sound. Rising from her stupor, she saw that down the short incline in front of them, a large, broad waterfall tumbled and roared over a wide shelf of rock into a foaming pool below.

"I've gone slightly off our route but I thought you'd like a swim." It was the first time he had spoken since their confrontation, his quiet voice sounding as if he was in pain. "Go on down, and I'll bring the towels," he added.

Silently, she opened the door and stumbled over the rocks towards the pool.

The water was very cold, but wonderfully refreshing after the hot, sticky journey. Emily swam around in mindless enjoyment, the roar of the waterfall filling her ears. Just why they had both shouted and tormented each other, for quite unnecessary reasons, was beyond her comprehension at the moment. She no longer felt that she hated him. She didn't, in fact, seem to feel anything at all. She was merely content just to cool her fevered body and leave any complicated thoughts until later.

She turned to see Ludo place his gun on a rock, ready for an emergency, before turning to enter the water. Emily gasped. She'd never seen a man totally naked before, and he looked... he looked magnificent! He was completely tanned all over, his broad shoulders seeming to fill her eyes as his powerful body gleamed in the brilliant light reflected off the water. The muscles in his heavy chest rippled as he picked his way over the dangerous rocks surrounding the pool on strong, tanned, muscular legs, so much longer than her own.

She felt herself grow hot. Her body was suddenly on fire with such a raging surge of desire, that confused and shaken, she dived beneath the water to cool off for a moment. Surfacing, she noticed that Ludo, who was swimming nearby, was saying something. She pointed to the waterfall behind her and then to her ears, shaking her head in a negative motion. "I can't hear you," she yelled, although it was obvious that he was unable to catch her words because of the waterfall's roar.

He swam slowly, very slowly towards her, coming to rest treading water in front of her trembling body. His large brown hands moved gently through the water as he placed them about her slim waist, drawing Emily towards him. She felt the tips of her breasts touch the fine black hairs of his chest, as he bent his dark, handsome head towards her, placing his mouth by her ear.

"Emily, you frightened me back by the ford. I thought you had been abducted." His hands tightened on her waist in tension. "Or killed," he added with a shudder.

She put her head back and looked into his sorrowful and tender eyes. What did it really matter what they had said and done to each other? She loved this man with every fibre of her being, and there was nothing she could do about it. Well, that wasn't entirely true, she thought idly as the water swirled and boiled about them. While she had been thinking about their relationship, her arms had, of their own volition, slowly wound themselves round his neck. Now she buried her hands in his hair as his head came slowly down towards her.

Emily closed her eyes as she felt their bodies meet, his hands slipping carefully and comfortingly about her. His mouth was gentle as he tenderly kissed the outline of her lips; soothing and comforting as he tasted their sweetness. Cradled in the security of his embrace, she felt him swim beneath an overhanging rock and his feet touch the shingled bottom of the pool.

"That's better!" he whispered in her ear with a small shaky laugh, and then as his lips slowly moved along her jaw line to find her mouth, she was lost. Lost as she floated weightless in his arms, his mouth moving sensually over her softly parted lips. Lost in delight as his hands slid erotically over her body before pressing her close to his naked form.

Suddenly it was over. Ludo lifted his head abruptly and stood rigid, every muscle tensed. She opened her eyes in dismay, and through pupils dilated by overwhelming desire, she saw a dark cloud pass overhead. Blinking rapidly, she realised that it wasn't a cloud; it was a helicopter!

"A helicopter means troops nearby," he said urgently in her ear, the waterfall still drowning their voices as it had masked the plane's arrival. "When I say 'go,' I want you to make for the towels over there by the rock, grab your clothes, and then run as fast as you can to the Land Rover. Okay? Climb inside—I'll be right behind you—I must collect the gun."

She nodded her understanding of his commands, and a few moments later Ludo gave her a small push. She made for the rocks as quickly as she could, seizing a towel and the rest of her things before running swiftly up the slope to the vehicle. She wrenched open her door and tumbled inside, only then knotting the dark green towel about her body.

A minute later he had joined her. "Don't be frightened, Emily. We'll get out of this somehow," he said, swiftly reaching for the second gun and placing the two rifles and a box of ammunition on the seat beside him.

"Frightened?" she said in a high clear voice she hardly recognised as her own. "I'm not frightened—I'm just damn angry with the mercenaries, or whoever they are! There we were, having...." She paused and blushed. "Well, I'm—I'm just very angry with them, that's all!"

"Darling Emily!" he laughed. "I knew I could rely on your ruthlessly selfish reactions! It's all right," he added quickly as she bridled. "I was only teasing. You're a great girl!" he smiled, stroking her cheek. "Now, to business. I estimate that we have only fifteen minutes, at the outside, before some troops are upon us. That helicopter was flying very low and in a searching pattern. They may well be looking for someone other than us—I very much hope that they are. However, discovery is certain I'm afraid, unless we move very swiftly indeed."

Ludo paused for a moment. "I'm going to run through our options. If you have a good idea, or you think I've missed something, for heaven's sake say so. Okay? Right. First the Land Rover. It must go I'm afraid. Our best bet is to push it into the pool. I think I've got enough time to weight it down with some large rocks. So that means that you must now nip into the back and pack what provisions you can—as light as possible please—and a pack containing our clothes. I will see to the guns and...."

"The waterfall!" she exclaimed, pointing excitedly. "Look, there seems to be a wide gap between the water and the rock wall behind. Isn't that a ledge running by the wall? Surely we could push the Land Rover...." Ludo leapt out, leaving her speaking to the empty air as he dashed for the waterfall. He stood looking at it for a moment, and then hurried back.

"Emily—I adore you! You clever, clever girl. Quick, move over into the driving seat and steer, while I push from behind." She waited, but nothing seemed to happen. Suddenly, his face peered in at the open window. He grasped her face and gave her a swift kiss. "The brake—you idiot!" he hissed, before disappearing to the back of the Land Rover.

Blushing and laughing, she released the brake and they made a slow progress down to the waterfall. The vehicle gathered momentum as the slope declined and Emily, her heart in her mouth, was relieved to find that the ledge was wider than it looked. Ludo pushed them to the far end of the ledge, as far away as possible from the opening. She slammed on the brake as he opened the rear door, seizing the camouflage net and draping the back of the vehicle as carefully as he could.

The driver's door seemed to be jammed hard against the rock wall behind the waterfall, whose noise was deafening. Emily looked out of the open window and found that although the base of the door was jammed, a foot higher there was another ledge cut into the rock.

It was about four feet wide and covered with some sort of lichen. She managed to climb out of the window and stood bouncing on what she discovered to be a deep layer of wet green moss, which felt as comfortable and spongy as a Dunlopillow mattress.

She walked along, touching Ludo's shoulder as he stood on the lower ledge making his final preparations to disguise the vehicle. "We can stand up here and sight the rifles along the roof of the Land Rover," she yelled in his ear. He nodded in agreement and she walked back, leaning in through the open window to haul out the guns and ammunition.

Ludo came and joined her up on the ledge, looking intently at her figure wrapped sarong style in the dark green towel. He bent inside the open window of the vehicle and removed something from the glove compartment. He pulled her to him and said in her ear, "Your hair's too bright," as he proceeded to stuff her wet and curly ash-blond hair inside a floppy, green army hat. He stepped back to check her appearance and Emily, feeling extraordinarily exhilarated despite their present danger, put a hand on her waist and wriggled her hips at him.

He grinned and slapped her behind, before tightening the soft green towel about his waist and going over to check his rifle. He put an arm about her waist as she went to stand beside him. "Don't fire unless I do," he yelled, "and then, don't bother with any fancy shots at the head—I want you to hit whoever it is plumb in the middle, and no messing about. Okay?"

Emily nodded, suddenly feeling very frightened indeed. She tried not to show it, but her hands trembled as she lifted her rifle, sighting it along the roof of the Land Rover. Ludo sensed her fear and held her close to him for a moment. "There's nothing to be ashamed of, if you're feeling frightened. We both are. That's the best way to stay alive," he whispered in her ear.

It seemed aeons of time passed as they waited, the roar of the waterfall deafening them. Maybe he was wrong, she thought. Maybe there are no mercenary troops near at all and this effort has been a waste of time. But his judgement had not betrayed him. She felt him tense beside her and a moment later she saw two Jeeps, with long waving radio aerials, drive into the clearing.

Men seemed to pour out from every direction. After her initial confusion she saw that there were only eight, dressed in jungle combat wear of green and brown shirts and long baggy trousers clamped into heavy boots. They seemed to be carrying a fearsome armoury of weapons, and Emily's heart sank as she wondered how, upon their discovery, she and Ludo could possibly defend themselves.

The black men stretched idly as they chatted together and lit cigarettes. It looked as if they were only there for a breather. Maybe they would soon go away. The tension was building up in her body and she felt enormously clear eyed, her senses tingling as the adrenalin flowed through her veins. The mercenaries seemed almost on the edge of departure, when there was a gesture from one of the men who had wandered down to the pool. Suddenly feeling sick with fright, Emily saw that he was holding up her shorts, the ones she had borrowed from Ludo, and which she must have dropped in her hasty dash to the Land Rover.

Emily put her hand over her mouth, glancing sideways at Ludo with stricken eyes. He shrugged and gave her a brief reassuring smile, before turning back to his telescopic sight. Emily prayed as she had never prayed before, watching the men gather around examining the soldier's find. One or two looked around the clearing and the pool, as if in search of the owner of the shorts.

Suddenly another Jeep arrived and a white man, dressed like the soldiers jumped out. He wore epaulettes on his shoulders and Emily guessed that he must be an officer. Looking at him through her telescopic sight, she thought he looked oddly familiar, and then realised that he had the same air of command and authority as Ludo. Waving to the men to follow him, he jumped back into the Jeep and roared off, swiftly followed by the soldiers.

Emily sagged against the Land Rover in relief. She had been so—so frightened. She didn't mind the whole world knowing that she, Emily Lambouchere, had been frightened to death! Suddenly feeling faint and weak, she turned towards Ludo, her limbs, which felt as heavy as lead, stumbling and slipping on the wet green moss. She clutched at him for support as her legs shot out from beneath her, catching him off balance. In a jumble of arms and legs, they fell on to the soft green cushion of moss, the towels falling from their bodies in the *mêlée*.

What happened next seemed somehow as inevitable as time itself. His mouth found her lips as his body pinned her to the soft ground beneath them, his heart beating as loudly as hers, his grey eyes clouded with rampant desire.

Their bodies, still shaking from the tension of the last half hour, began to tremble at each other's touch. Sensation followed intense sensation at each delicious movement of their bodies. They were both totally, wonderfully, and magnificently out of control, shaken by the urgency of their mutual passion. Emily felt the blood pounding in her head, and she knew that she would either go mad or die with her fierce longing for Ludo, when he took her in a sweeping tide of such storming intensity that she felt she was indeed dying—dying of rapture. As he raised her to the very peak of sexual fulfilment, she shook and sobbed with joy in his arms.

Later, much later, she awoke to find herself lying

What made Marge burn the toast and miss her favorite soap opera?

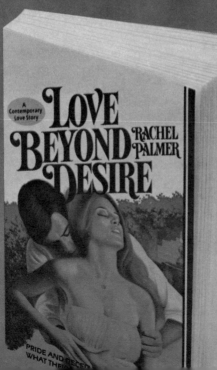

A Contemporary Love Story

LOVE BEYOND DESIRE

RACHEL PALMER

...At his touch, her body felt a familiar wild stirring, but she struggled to resist it. This is not love, she thought bitterly.

PRIDE AND PREC...
WHAT THE...

A compelling love story of mystery and intrigue... conflicts and jealousies... and a forbidden love that threatens to shatter the lives of all involved with the aristocratic Lopez family.

↙ Mail this card today for your FREE gifts.

TAKE THIS BOOK
AND TOTE BAG FREE!

Mail to: **SUPERROMANCE**
2504 W. Southern Avenue, Tempe, Arizona 85282

YES, please send me FREE and without any obligation, my SUPERROMANCE novel, *Love Beyond Desire*. If you do not hear from me after I have examined my FREE book, please send me the 4 new SUPERROMANCE books every month as soon as they come off the press. I understand that I will be billed only $2.50 per book (total $10.00). There are no shipping and handling or any other hidden charges. There is no minimum number of books that I have to purchase. In fact, I may cancel this arrangement at any time. *Love Beyond Desire* and the tote bag are mine to keep as FREE gifts even if I do not buy any additional books.

134-CIS-KAF6

Name	(Please Print)	
Address		Apt. No.
City		
State		Zip
Signature	(If under 18, parent or guardian must sign.)	

This offer is limited to one order per household and not valid to present subscribers. We reserve the right to exercise discretion in granting membership. If price changes are necessary you will be notified. Offer expires March 31, 1984.

PRINTED IN U.S.A.

SUPERROMANCE ™

naked inside the Land Rover, with Ludo asleep beside her. She had only a dim recollection of his picking her up in his arms after the passionate explosion between them. *He must have carried me in here*, she thought in bewilderment, gazing with shining eyes at the man she loved so deeply. The interior of the vehicle was lit by a dim green light, the sun's rays being filtered by the curtain of water which flowed past the windows of the Land Rover. It seemed so safe and warm as she crawled over to Ludo. At the touch of her body he moved lazily in his sleep, his arms clasping her possessively to him as she sighed with contentment and fell asleep again.

Emily surfaced to feel Ludo's hands gently moving over her body. She stretched lazily and smiled up at him as he looked down at her, his eyes containing both tender desire and hesitation. "My darling—I can't keep my hands off you," he murmured huskily. "We ought to go. I...."

She smiled lovingly as the centuries-old instinct born into women came to her aid. "Ludo," she whispered, her hands stroking his broad bare shoulders, her fingers gently ruffling the curly dark hair on his tanned chest. "Oh Ludo," she breathed as she gently caressed him, lower and lower, moving her body slowly and sensually beneath him.

"For heaven's sake!" he protested thickly, his breath becoming ragged and uneven. "Emily—don't tempt me! I can't help myself. I... Oh, how you tempt me!"

She reached up, winding her fingers in his dark hair and glorying in the knowledge that she could arouse him as he was arousing her. Slowly drawing his head down towards her, her mouth effectively silenced his protests. He parted her soft lips, savouring the inner sweetness and groaning in anguish as her hands continued to intimately and wantonly caress his body.

Movement, time and place became a blur as their bodies, on fire with mutual passion, clung together. He slowly withdrew his mouth and looked down at Emily, her eyes gazing up at him from the deep depths of desire. He smoothed the curly locks from her brow, and began to make love to her slowly and with infinite tenderness. She was overcome with one exquisite sensation after another, as he kissed and caressed her body, bringing her to such a pitch of longing that she moaned, begging for fulfilment. Only then did he allow his own passion to rein freely, raising them both to the dizzy heights of an emotional intensity such as she had never believed possible. Emily cried out, as great waves rocked and shook her frame, and they climaxed together in a mutual explosion of raging passion.

EMILY LAY IN HER LONELY BED that night, her limps aching from the hard day's drive, and from her passionate lovemaking with Ludo that morning. She could hardly believe it was only this morning that they had made such glorious, fantastically exciting love. It didn't seem possible that she could have been raised to such heights, only to be dashed on the rocks again so swiftly.

They had fallen asleep after their lovemaking and had awoken later in the early afternoon. They had been so busy pushing the Land Rover out from beneath the waterfall and winching it back up to the clearing, that it had taken her some time to realise that all was not well. It wasn't anything that Ludo said; he had been very complimentary about her idea of hiding the Land Rover and for her courage and lack of fear in the face of the enemy. It was just that something was not quite right . . . maybe it was her imagination.

It wasn't her imagination, she realised, as the day went on. Ludo was polite, helpful and friendly, but there was a barrier, a wall between them. His clear grey eyes were remote and impersonal, as it became increasingly obvious that he deeply regretted what had happened between them. There was no tension. There was...there was nothing. It was far more intimidating than his anger would have been, and she began to shrivel up inside.

"Where—where are we going now?" she asked in a small voice, after an hour's silence. An hour in which she had been occupied with her own unhappy thoughts.

"I've had to change our route," he answered quietly. "It now means that we must go through part of the rain forest, and I'm going for some constructive help. I know you're tough, Emily—" he smiled briefly sideways at her "—but we can't take the Land Rover through the virgin forest. It is going to mean porters to carry our supplies, and that's what I'm hoping to arrange by calling in on a friend of mine."

She nodded in understanding, and then for the rest of the journey, she lapsed back into a miasma of confused thoughts and remembrances. There was, after all, no way she could hide the fact that she had, well, practically seduced Ludo, the second time they made love. He—he had been betrayed by his body's urgency for her, but his mind had been unwilling. She had to face the fact, however unpleasant she found it.

She began to consider the ways and means by which she could possibly contrive that they should repeat their morning's lovemaking. Ludo was right, she acknowledged ruefully and honestly, for the first time in her life. She was spoilt. She had always taken what she had wanted; there was no gainsaying the fact. Maybe at twenty she was too old to change? Whatever the reason, she wanted him. She wanted him now, in the future and forever, and she was going to manage it somehow. She had to! Without Ludo by her side, life was going to hold no meaning whatsoever.

Glancing at his sharply etched face beside her, she sighed inwardly. She didn't think much of her chances, if she was honest. But she had to try, she had to fight for the man who had suddenly become the most important being in the world to her.

The sun was setting, as they rolled over a wooden bridge set over a gorge, and came to rest in the middle of a small African village. "Stay here," he said and then he jumped down and walked slowly into the middle of the deserted clearing. He was suddenly surrounded by tiny men, each about four and a half feet tall, wearing loincloths and carrying bows and arrows.

Ludo began speaking to them in a language that Emily hadn't heard before. Two of them ran off to a hut at the back of the clearing, which Emily saw was much bigger than the other small rounded huts. Gradually, women emerged followed by children, who ran and danced around the Land Rover. Emily sat inside, wishing that Ludo would come back.

There was a sudden bellow of laughter as a large African emerged from the big hut, dressed in beige trousers and a white shirt. He walked towards Ludo with his hands outstretched. Emily's mouth dropped open, as she listened to the exchange between the two men. "Hi there—you stuck-up man!" he shouted in an upper-class accent.

"Hi there, yourself—you stranger!" laughed Ludo, as the two men embraced.

Ludo led the man back to the Land Rover. "I very much hope that you'll let us stay the night," he said. "I've got a passenger, and we need your help."

"Why Ludovic!" the man bellowed. "What have you here?" he laughed. "Well—this must be the most beau-ti-ful girl I've seen you with in years!"

Emily smiled nervously as he opened the door and helped her to descend.

"Emily, I'd like you to meet Dr. James Martin, doctor of medicine and anthropologist. This is Miss Emily Lambouchere, James," said Ludo.

"Lambouchere? The Lambouchere Mines...?" Dr. Martin said.

"Yes," replied Ludo shortly.

"I am delighted—not to say enchanted, Miss Lambouchere," Dr. Martin said with a perfect accent, raising her hand to his lips. His friendly smile did much to restore her confidence as he led them toward the large hut.

"Well, old boy," James Martin drawled. "I'm very pleased to see you both. From what I can gather from the confused accounts on Zaire radio—there's been a complete radio shut-down here in Ouanda—things seemed to have been a bit bloody up at the mine."

"They were, rather. We are, as you might say, on the run."

"I gathered that, old boy. Where are you making for? The Cameroon?"

"Hopefully," replied Ludo. "We'll have to go through the rain forest, and I want to borrow some porters. Have you still got those three Bantu porters around?"

"Can do." Dr. Martin looked sternly at his friend. "But I want them back in good order, Ludo. Not half-starved and full of dysentery like after your last trip through the Congo rain forest."

"This should only take two or three days, James. That last trip was months, and I came back in the same condition as well, you know."

"Don't I just! Miss Lambouchere," he said, opening the door of the hut, "won't you come in?"

"Please call me Emily," she replied, smiling at Dr. Martin, "and I'll call you James, if I may."

"Absolutely!" he agreed.

The hut had a grass patio at the back. Emily thought it was the height of sheer luxury to sit in the relative cool of the evening, looking out at a small stream and the forest at the back. James poured them both a large whisky and told Emily about his work with the pygmies. Half-way through their conversation, there was a deputation of short men at the door. James came back laughing.

"They want to know if your hair is really that colour!"

"Tell them yes," she smiled. "Just as well, really. I wouldn't have been able to do anything about dying the roots on this journey!"

"You know, Ludo," James said. "Miss Emily here is not at all what I expected. I...er...." He turned to her. "I really thought you would be very different."

"I probably was," she said quietly. "I—I seem to have learnt a lot on this journey." James Martin looked quickly at his two visitors and, keeping his thoughts to himself, changed the subject.

"I think we should raise our glasses to the dear departed," he said, pouring them both another tot of whisky. "To Miss Emily Lambouchere, who apparently died so tragically at the diamond mine, and to Dr. Ludovic Vandenberg who has, so it seems, completely disappeared. The news was carried with all the authority of the BBC Overseas Service. Of course," he laughed, "I'm a great believer in resurrection, myself!"

With enormous kindness, he had fed them both and arranged for the porters to be on hand first thing in the morning. He had also arranged for a tent to be set up by his small patio. "I insist that the lady has the only spare room," James had said, "unless...?" He raised an eyebrow in Ludo's direction, and seeing his friend shake his head, had continued smoothly, "Unless Ludo insists on making Emily sleep outside. But I'm sure he's too much of a gentleman for that."

"You are quite right," Ludo agreed firmly.

Emily, who had missed none of the exchange between the two men, rose quietly a few minutes later to say good-night.

She lay unhappily in her bed, so soft after the hard benches of the Land Rover, listening to the faint background noise as the two men talked in the other room.

She thought about the events of the day, blushing at the memory of how lovingly and wantonly she had caressed every inch of Ludo's firm body. He had murmured his delight at her ardent response to the urgency of his lips and hands, the intensity of her overwhelming passion. She grew hot and feverish, moving restlessly on the unaccustomed luxury of a spring mattress. She remembered how, when she was at fever pitch and pleading for his complete possession, he had raised himself to allow his eyes to drink in the curving swell of her breasts, the soft skin of her stomach and the long, tender line of her thighs, before he had groaned helplessly, losing what little control he had left as his legs had parted hers.

Damp with perspiration from the hot, humid night, Emily prayed fervently that Ludo would come to love her as she loved him. Surely it couldn't just be lust for her that he felt. She hoped that somehow God would grant her prayer.

She woke during the night. As she tried to orient herself, staring into the unfamiliar darkness, she realised that the sounds which had awakened her had been her own miserably helpless tears.

CHAPTER SIX

THE NEXT MORNING, Ludo, Emily and their three African porters entered the hot, humid and perpetual gloom of the Ouandan rain forest.

"It looks so much cooler and pleasant down there," Emily had said of the forest as she, Ludo and James Martin had breakfasted together earlier that morning. The two men had laughed wryly as Ludo had risen to see to the packing of their equipment. "Make the most of the fresh air up here," he had warned her. "It will be the last time for some days that you will feel fit and well."

Left alone with James, she had turned to him with questioning eyes. "Most sensible people," he told her, "avoid the rain forest like the plague. I'm not trying to put you off; you'll be able to sample its delights soon enough!" He poured them some more coffee. "You'll be all right with Ludo, Emily. Our zoologist friend knows all the problems and pitfalls that travel through rain forests can bring. He'll look after you—don't worry."

"I'm sure he will," she murmured, sipping the hot liquid. "Have—have you known him long?"

"Long enough. We shared a set of rooms at Cambridge, where I was studying medicine—my interest in anthropology came later. We've bumped into each other fairly regularly ever since. Ludo's a great guy, only..." he paused, looking at her intently.

"Only don't get too fond of him, will you?" James said quietly.

Emily looked at him startled, and bit her lip. "Is it so very obvious?" she asked, her face hot with embarrassment.

James laughed, but warmly and kindly. "My dear girl, I am a doctor. We're supposed to be good at diagnostics! However, there is—how shall I put it—a fair amount of electric tension about you two, that even a blind man couldn't miss."

She blushed, and bent her head down looking at her cup. "Why—why shouldn't I get too fond of him?" she asked quietly. "Is—is he married?" It had only just occurred to her that he might be, and she suddenly felt sick with nervous apprehension.

"No—not any more. He got married just after coming down from Cambridge. The whole short affair was a disaster, and he's been strictly solo ever since." He gazed kindly at the slim woman looking so woebegone in front of him.

"He was very young, and the whole business shattered him. It isn't that he doesn't like women; even I as a mere male can see that with his looks the women are after him like bees after a honey-pot! He's had masses of affairs, but he always says he'll never love anyone, ever again—and maybe he's right."

"I—I don't believe you can ever say that, about anyone," she said stubbornly.

"You may be right, Emily," he sighed. "But you've got a real problem with him—you especially. Take my advice, most kindly meant and sincerely given. Don't fall in love with him. You'll only give yourself a great deal of heartache and distress."

Your advice has come too damn late, she thought. "Why me especially?" she asked, recalling his words.

"Because of the girl he married—Adrienne Mortimer. Old Lord Mortimer's daughter. You must have heard of her—in your circles anyway."

"Oh, no!" Emily looked at him with stricken eyes. So that was why Ludo had been so harsh and rude to her when they'd first met! Adrienne Mortimer's marital progress through the royal and semi-royal houses of Europe, as she married and discarded husbands with monotonous regularity had earned her the nickname of "The Bolter." The rich and spoilt daughter of Lord Mortimer, the newspaper proprietor, she had been a prominent member of the international jet-set for many years. Finally ending up with a Greek shipping millionaire, she had been found dead from an overdose of sleeping pills two years ago.

"You've got a real problem on your hands, Emily," he said with a kind smile. "I think you're a great girl, and so indeed does Ludo. He was singing your praises last night in no uncertain manner. But, always in the context of your background, I'm afraid. You've proved to be far more capable and resilient than he could ever have imagined. However, he will never be able to forget, even if you can, the world from which you come. He's got a real chip on his shoulder about it, and it's been there for a long time. I'm sorry...."

"Oh, James," she moaned, burying her face in her hands. "What shall I do?"

"What you're going to do right now," he said briskly, "is to let me give you a quick medical inspection; Ludo's idea, and a good one. After that," he shrugged, "get through this journey, and then go home and forget him in the best way you know how. It's the only reasonable suggestion I can offer, I'm afraid."

"Well, my boy," James said later, as Ludo came back to join them. "I am pleased to tell you that Miss Lambouchere is in far better condition than I suspect you are—a very fit specimen indeed. I've put together a medical pack for you. Don't forget to check it fairly soon, so you know what you've got. Okay?"

"Okay," said Ludo, shaking his hand. "I'm damn

grateful, James. Look after the Land Rover, I'll be back for it one day soon I hope. Time we were off, Emily," he said, turning to have a word with the three African porters.

"Goodbye James," she said, taking his hand, and then put her arms around him, kissing his cheek. "You've been so kind," she smiled sadly at him. "thank you for your good advice. It's a bit late, but I'll try to heed it."

Now, as their party entered the forest, Emily momentarily forgot her troubles as she looked about her with interest. The jungle was totally different to the way she had imagined, and she was amazed by the scale of the gigantic trees which soared over her head. Some of them were as wide as a house, with thick visible roots, almost the size of the Land Rover.

It was like being inside some very large and dark cathedral, the high soaring navelike branches meeting over their heads hundreds of feet above. The canopy of the large trees completely blocked the light, and they picked their way carefully over the ground littered with fallen leaves and pieces of wood. It was dark, dim and eerie. So still and quiet. There were occasional bird calls and screeches from monkeys, but otherwise the air hung heavy and profoundly still.

And it was hot! Far hotter than on the savannah plains over which they had been travelling. It's like some enormous Turkish bath, Emily thought, as she looked about her in the twilight of the forest, breathing in the humid and heavy air. There was every kind of tree and creeper, but very few flowers, and those that she saw were pale. White or greenish orchids grew on the branches of trees, and huge fungi spread out from the tree trunks like giant saucers.

Emily had also expected the forest to be denser than it was. They walked along freely, if carefully because of the dim light. She might have expected the floor of the jungle to be full of decay, but it was surprisingly firm, and although the air was humid, it had a neutral smell. The most outstanding characteristic, she soon found, was that everything was wringing wet. The trunks of the trees ran with water as did the vines and leaves. There was a constant drip from the leaves above, and soon she and the rest of the party were soaking wet as well.

"This will make your hair curl—literally," Ludo laughed, as he waited for her to catch him up.

"Don't mention it," she groaned. "I look just like Shirley Temple already! And please," she begged him with a faint smile, "please don't say that I'm looking pretty either. Since I haven't a mirror, I'm concentrating on trying to think of myself as I used to look—before all this!" she gestured around her.

She could have bitten out her tongue, as his face closed up, the blank look coming back into his eyes. "Never mind, Emily," he said blandly. "We'll have you back in civilization before long."

With unhappy painful eyes, she watched him stride off to confer with their porters. Why couldn't she have kept her damn mouth shut, she thought bitterly as she trudged after him.

They had been going only for an hour or two, before she began to feel oppressed. It wasn't just because of her feelings for Ludo, she realised. It was as if the forest was an enormously hot, dark womb, from which there seemed no escape. Feelings of claustrophobic panic began to cloud her mind.

As if guessing how she was feeling, Ludo came back and walked beside her, helping her over some of the larger fallen branches on the ground. He talked determinedly and firmly, as if trying to banish her fears, and she was grateful to him for his kindness.

"This is a primeval forest," he explained. "What you might call virgin territory. That's the only reason we can get through it. Where clearings of the forest have occurred and the jungle has taken over again, it becomes totally impossible to get through what naturalists call the secondary growth."

"Will we see any of your gorillas?" she asked. "Or don't they like this sort of area?"

"They love it!" he smiled. "They're vegetarians, and live on a diet of leaves and shoots. I haven't seen any of their spoor yet, but I'll let you know when we do.

"Although it is referred to in this country as Ouandan, this is really part of the Congo rain forest, which stretches thousands of miles right across Africa. You've heard of Stanley?" he asked.

"Yes," she replied. "My great-great-grandfather was on the journey with him along the Congo River from Zanzibar to the Atlantic Ocean in 1874." She smiled at his look of surprise.

"Don't look so amazed, Ludo," she said with some asperity. "How do you think my family came to have investments in Ouanda?"

"I should have realised, of course," he said slowly. "I just somehow assumed that your ancestors had been amongst the first French settlers."

"I've got old Pierre Lambouchere's diary at home," explained Emily. "It really is a fascinating document. I spent hours reading it as a child. He and Stanley—of Stanley and 'Dr. Livingstone, I presume' fame—they were partners. Apparently their journey was financed by newspapers in their two countries, and the whole trip took them 999 days. It's an easy figure to remember!" she smiled.

"They were great friends, and buddies," Emily continued, "and so when Stanley was commissioned by the then king of Belgium—Leopold something or other—two years later, to buy or acquire the Congo, old great-great-grandfather Pierre went along too."

"How did Pierre Lambouchere land up in Ouanda?" Ludo asked, intrigued by the tale.

"I'm not entirely sure what happened. Apparently the two men quarrelled, and so he left Stanley, who was busy grabbing the Congo for Belgium, and went north to Ouanda, and did some grabbing of his own—for France—and himself!" she laughed. "Really those old Victorian explorers were amazing. Fancy trying to seize an African country nowadays! Mind you," she added seriously, "his diary makes awful reading. That trip down the Congo River—the first in history—was a terrible experience. He and Stanley lost nearly all their men. Only a few of the original party were left alive at the end of the day. Crocodiles, rampant fevers, the lot!" She shuddered.

"It sounds fascinating," he said. "You're very lucky to have such a diary—what a fantastic record of such an epic journey it must be."

"I'll tell you what Ludo." Emily was struck by a sudden thought. "If you get us out of here—this damn country I mean—I'll give it to you. It would be a small price to pay for all you've done, after all."

"Oh, no!" he said firmly. "I couldn't possibly accept it."

Emily shrugged. She would give it to him; she'd made up her mind on that. There wasn't any point in arguing about it in the meantime. She walked along feeling somewhat happier, knowing that she could give the man she loved something he would truly value.

They trudged on for the rest of the day, making reasonable if slow progress. Reaching a small clearing late in the afternoon, Ludo called a halt, and the three African porters set about unloading themselves and erecting tents. Half-way through they heard a growl of thunder, and minutes later they were all drenched by a torrential rain storm, the drops being so dense and heavy that they stung the skin.

Diving for shelter, Emily stood unhappily amongst some ferns as she leant against a large tree, agreeing wholeheartedly with James Martin's view that the forest was to be avoided like the plague! An hour later, the rain stopped as abruptly as it had started. Soaked and feeling miserable, Emily went to see if there was anything she could usefully do to help.

"We'd better see to your legs," Ludo remarked, as he directed the re-erection of the tents, now steaming in the sun which filtered down on to the clearing.

"My legs?" she asked, and looked down briefly, before giving a scream of horror.

"Ah...." she cried, trembling and shaking. "Wh—what are they...?" She covered her eyes, unable to look as she jumped up and down, trying to shake off the large black sluglike things clinging to her legs.

"Calm down, Emily!" Ludo said sharply. "They're only leeches."

"Only leeches!" she screamed. "Get them off... get them off at once! Oh, Ludo...!" She trembled in disgust and terror.

"Sit down and calm down." Ludo put an arm around her shoulder. "I'll just go and get one of my cigars to burn them off."

"Why—why have you got to burn the—the horrid things off?" she asked, her teeth still chattering as she shuddered in revulsion. "Why can't you just pull them out—Oh, Ludo—they look so awful!"

"Because, if I pull them out, part of the head might remain lodged in your flesh, and could cause an infection—that's why," he said calmly, lighting his cigar.

She turned her head away, as he performed the necessary removal of the blood-swollen leeches. "Now," he said, "that didn't hurt, did it? In fact, you didn't know they were on your legs till I pointed it out."

Her only reply was to shudder and clasp her eyes tightly shut, in order to avoid looking at the loathsome creatures. "I'd better lend you a pair of my trousers tomorrow," he said, with a smile at her expression.

"Oh, yes—please!" she said thankfully, getting up, and moving over to the tents.

Kanaki, one of the Bantu porters, proudly showed her the tent designed for her sole use. "You be nice and safe here, missy," he said. "Why your husband no sleep with you? Is not good."

Emily felt too tired and emotionally exhausted to begin to try and explain that she and Ludo weren't married. She sat inside her little tent for a while, feeling lonely and unhappy. There was no doubt at all in her mind that Ludo was deliberately erecting a thick wall between them, brick by brick. As the days went by, it would become more and more impossible for her to break it down, and there seemed nothing she could do.

No wonder Ludo had taken such a strong aversion to her the first time they had met. Even she, very much younger than his ex-wife, had heard the stories about Adrienne Mortimer. "Bolting" from one man to another, breaking up many happy marriages as she had capriciously selected and discarded her husbands. The two constant remarks used when describing her had been: "Fabulously beautiful" and "a prize bitch."

Her heart was wrung with love and compassion for the young man Ludo had once been. Adrienne must have wounded him irreparably. James Martin had said that his short marriage had shattered Ludo, but he would also undoubtedly judge other women by Adrienne's exquisite loveliness.

Emily sighed with despondency. Not only had Ludo reacted so sharply to her name and obvious wealth, but she knew she couldn't hold a candle to his ex-wife's beauty. There was nothing she could do about her own looks, Emily decided. Especially here in the jungle, with not a scrap of make-up within miles. The thought of a hairdresser and make-up artist suddenly materialising here, in the rain forest, gave her the only smile of the day.

What could she possibly do to prove that she was capably of being more, far more, than a silly little rich girl? She had learnt to love and trust him—to trust him with her life, in fact. Something she could never have contemplated happening to her, not in a million years. Certainly not to the super-cool Emily Lambouchere who had viewed life around her with bored, uncaring eyes....

Emily writhed with embarrassment at just how stupid and tiresome she must have seemed, especially to those like Ludo, who existed outside her boring world. She couldn't blame him for recoiling from her at the beginning of their acquaintance; but surely now that he knew her better...now that he must know how much she cared for him...?

Clenching her teeth with frustration, Emily swore under her breath. She needed time in order to break down the barriers that Ludo was erecting between them. And time—that most fleeting and elusive quantity—time was fast running out on her like sand in an hourglass.

"Supper, Emily," Ludo called. She crawled reluctantly out of her tent and walked slowly over to the fire.

"You're right," Ludo said, as they sat holding their mugs of coffee at the end of the meal. "You do look just like Shirley Temple—but I hasten to add, not at all pretty...."

"Thanks," she said, dryly, trying to look at him with disinterest, and only succeeding in thinking how the surrounding environment suited his rugged good looks.

"If you'd let me finish," he said slowly. "I was going to add that I thought you looked very beautiful." He gazed at the woman who without a trace of make-up still managed to light up the jungle with her luminous beauty. Emily felt her pale skin, slightly tanned from their journey, flush at his words. Her hands began to tremble as her repressed, frustrated longing for his embrace seemed to become almost more than she could bear.

"But not beautiful enough, it seems!" she cried bitterly. Jumping to her feet, she threw her mug angrily on to the ground before swiftly running off towards her tent.

Ludo followed her departure with blank eyes, turning back to stare into the fire for some time. Sighing, he rose and walked slowly over to her tent, set beside his own.

"Emily...?" he called softly. "Are you all right?"

"No, I'm not all right!" She sat in a miserable huddled heap on the ground, her back to the closed tent flap. "Go away. I—I don't want to talk to you. Go away!"

There was a pause, and then she heard his footsteps retreating towards the fire. He can't get anything right can he, she thought in angry frustration. Surely he knew I wanted him to come in and comfort me? I hate him...I love him...oh, what shall I do, she wailed silently, as she buried her face in her hands and lay trembling with misery on her sleeping bag.

That night she dreamed again the nightmare which had haunted her all her life. She was running. Running till her lungs almost seemed to burst with exhaustion, as she ran down the long drive of her old home. The car ahead was going faster and faster as Emily called, "Come back...come back, mummy... oh, please, come back!" But there was no reply as the vehicle increased its speed. Just a wave of a white arm as the car turned the corner and was lost to sight. Great racking sobs shook her frame as she fell to the ground exhausted. "Come back...come back," she cried, the tears running down her face....

"It's all right, darling. It's all right, Emily...."
Ludo's warm and tender arms were about her, as she
woke to find herself sobbing in his embrace. "She
didn't come back...she never came back." She could
do nothing to prevent the tears flowing down her
cheeks in a steady stream as Ludo soothed and com-
forted her, rocking her in his arms like a baby.

"Everything's going to be all right," he murmured,
wiping her tears away by the light of the storm lantern
he had brought into the tent.

At last her sobs subsided and she lay exhausted in his
arms, savouring the musky male smell of his skin, the
total comfort of his embrace.

"Poor Emily." He tenderly stroked the hair from her
damp, perspiring brow. "You seem to be haunted by
bad dreams. Very often in the night I've heard you crying. But by the time I've woken up properly and gone
to see to you, you've been fast asleep again. Is it always
the same recurring nightmare?" he asked gently.

She nodded, her head buried in his shoulder.

"Why don't you tell me about it?" he said. "It might
help."

"Oh, no—I can't..." she protested, beginning to
shake again.

"Yes, you can," Ludo said firmly, turning her face
towards him.

"But I don't want to remember it again... I don't!"
she cried anxiously, gazing up to find his grey eyes
filled with compassion. "It's—it's just a dream, that's
all. It...it would sound so stupid to...to talk about. It's
only a dream, Ludo," she repeated, "just a silly
dream...."

"Look Emily, you've obviously got some sort of
problem that is being suppressed during your waking
hours, and which is finding release when you are
asleep." He looked down into her confused and fright-

ened eyes. "You don't have to be a psychiatrist to know that it helps to talk it over with someone else—it really does," he assured her.

"I..." she shrugged, and sighed helplessly. 'I went to see someone like that once," she said slowly. "He charged me one hundred guineas and told me I had a mother fixation—or something. There—there didn't seem much point in going back, somehow..." her voice trailed away.

"Tell me about your mother, Emily," Ludo said softly, as he began rhythmically and soothingly to stroke her back. "Tell me all about it."

She sighed and closed her eyes, the comfort of his touch helping her tense muscles to relax. "It's an awfully common story, really it is," she said slowly. "I don't suppose it was all her fault, not entirely. My father was very peculiar; there's no doubt about that." Emily sighed, remembering the large, dark gloomy house whose walls, covered in heavy oak panelling, had always seemed to close in on her as a young child.

"He...my father...he was a lot older than my mother. Poor papa," she murmured, as she began to tentatively retrace her steps down the long corridor of childhood memories. "He was always such a sad, lonely figure. He was the youngest of a large family, all living in Paris at the start of the Second World War," she explained. "I don't know much about it, but soon after the Germans occupied France, he and his English nanny came back from a walk, one morning, to find a group of Gestapo troops in the house. His mother, father, sisters and brothers were all being bundled into a lorry. He never saw them again."

Emily pushed a hand distractedly through her hair. "I remember how tears used to fill his eyes when he spoke about it. He was only a little boy, and he had to stand on the opposite side of the road, Nanny White's hand over his mouth to stop him screaming, as he watched his mother being beaten as she tried to climb up into the van. It must have been awful Ludo, really awful!"

He held her closer to him, as she continued. "Nanny White managed to get them to England somehow. I can just remember her, Ludo. I used to think she was a fearsome old dragon, but my father adored her. She contacted some friends of the family, and for the rest of his childhood they shuffled around to various friends and distant relatives, never having any permanent home. After the war," she sighed, "he never found any of his family again. They had all been interned or sent to the labour camps...one way and another they all perished. All because of the diamonds, papa said." Emily buried her head in Ludo's shoulder. "Papa said that some of the Nazi High Command were looking ahead to the end of a victorious war, and the expansion of German colonialism in Africa." Her voice was muffled as she added, "He always said his life had been ruined by the diamonds. That they were unlucky for our family and...and I believe him. It looks as if they're going to ruin my life, as well—one way and another." She sniffed and rubbed her eyes, brushing away the tears which threatened to fall again.

"Life is what you make it, Emily," Ludo said gently. "You really mustn't blame inanimate objects for things that happen. It's going to be up to you whether you make a success of your life or not." He laid her back gently on her sleeping bag. "I'm going off to make us a cup of tea. I'll be back in a moment. Okay?"

She nodded, and lay looking at the moths and mosquitos circling around the lantern he had left behind, buried deep in thought. Her poor father had been weak, and on going up to Oxford had made books his only world. A world of Old Norse mythology.

"I've had a lot of time to think on this journey," she said as Ludo returned, placing a hot mug in her hands.

"I—I think that just as I escaped into what the gossip columns call 'the mad social whirl,' so my father escaped into books. I'm told that he wasn't too communicative before, but after my mother ran away...well he just became a recluse. He was never—never quite there, if you know what I mean. He'd look at you, and nod and smile, but he was somehow miles and miles away, with Thor and Woden and all his other mythical gods, which were far more real to him than I was," she said sadly.

"Your mother...?" he prompted holding her hand and gently rubbing the soft skin of her inner wrist with his thumb.

Emily shrugged her shoulders. Only an almost imperceptible tightening of her hand in his, betraying her inner tension.

"My mother was the youngest daughter of a mad old Scottish laird. Her family had ruled their Highland estate for hundreds of years, and held themselves accountable to no one. Great-grandfather Murray," she gave him a faint, wry smile, "it was said, used to shoot pheasants and peasants with equal impartiality! They're all as mad as hatters. I go and stay with them, now and then, and honestly the old castle is like living in Transylvania! The place is stuffed full of aged relatives. You should see some of the old aunts, wandering around in long flowing dresses, muttering to themselves. You'd expect Count Dracula to appear any moment!" She smiled gratefully at him as he laughed at the picture she had drawn. His strong, normal personality was helping to dispel the atmosphere of her nightmare, traces of which still clung to the edges of her mind.

"Anyway," she continued, "my parents' marriage was a disaster from the start. My mother, having managed to escape from her crazy family set-up, wasn't prepared to settle down with someone so like the people she'd left behind. As I said, I can't...I can't blame her, really. She stuck it out until I was five, and then ran away. She's still running as far as I know. She's had five husbands at the last count. I think the present one is a Mexican dress designer...."

Emily's voice became hard and brittle. "I really don't know what she's doing at the moment. I haven't seen her since I was fifteen, at my father's funeral."

"Poor Emily...."

"My dear man," she drawled, in a voice she hadn't used since that night at the mine. "It happens all the time. James Martin told me about your wife. It's a common story, isn't it? After all, far worse things happen in this world. Think of all the people shoved into orphanages," she said wryly, "or given to foster parents who treat them badly. I was lucky, I suppose. I was surrounded by wealth and privilege—anything I wanted I could have...."

"Anything except caring love," he said softly.

Emily shrugged, and was silent for some time, staring sightlessly into the blackness outside the opening of the tent. "I think... I think what I minded so much," she said slowly, "was that she didn't take me with her. I—I had to live in that frighteningly dark, ugly pile of a house, never even seeing much of my father. My only friends were the servants, really...."

"You must have seen your mother sometimes." Ludo put a comforting arm about her.

"No, I didn't." She shook her head. "I was packed off, at the age of seven to a boarding school, and I didn't see her again, until my father died of cancer. Not until the day of his funeral. I'll—I'll never forget that day. Never..." she sighed, shivering.

"It was so cold and damp. Right in the middle of February... isn't it extraordinary how some images or smells bring memories flooding back? I think it must have been the dripping water from the leaves, here in the forest, that has brought it all back to me, so—so vividly. It was foggy and grey that morning, I remember; the steady downpour had soaked us all as we stood by my father's grave at the end of the service."

Emily gave a harsh laugh. "You should have seen me. I had been let out of school for a few days, and I was wearing the ghastly school uniform, which was far too short because I'd done another spurt of growing. Even at fifteen I seemed to tower over most of the other mourners. My hair was all wet and curly from the rain, and I—I suppose I was looking pretty dreadful." Her hands clutched Ludo's, her knuckles white with tension.

"Suddenly—there she was! My mother, I mean. Looking so smart and sophisticated, dressed all in bright red. I remember...I remember that the colour seemed so shocking, somehow, with everyone else in dark clothes. She had a tall, blond, handsome young man with her, holding the umbrella, and I—I can remember staring at them open-mouthed as they walked up the path of the churchyard. I—I wasn't sure it was her, you see. I mean, I—I hadn't seen her since I was five. It had been so long...."

Emily began to shake, her eyes glazed as she became part of the scene so long ago. "You must be little Emily, I suppose?" Her voice took on the timbre of a clipped, brittle accent, as she relived her mother's words. "My dear—what a fright you look! And so ugly!"

Emily began to shake with tension. "Do you know what she said next, Ludo? It's sure to make you laugh," she said breathlessly. "She said—she said, 'I did wonder, sometimes, whether I should have left you behind with your dotty old father. But now I see I did absolutely the right thing. My dear, I wouldn't be seen dead with such an ugly, scrawny brat like you.'"

Ludo's arms were strong about her as she sobbed into his shoulder. "My mother went away and left me," she cried, torn by sobs that shook her slim frame, "and—and then came back and rejected me again!"

Ludo rocked her gently in his arms, whispering endearments into her soft curly hair. Presently Emily stopped shaking and lay quiet. "I've never told anyone about that, before," she said slowly. "It hurt too much, I suppose."

"Emily," he said, his voice low and tender. "Many people are prisoners of their childhood. Something happens that marks them for life. Now, I study animal life, and what raises us humans above the animal kingdom is the ability to think, logically and clearly. We have been born with free will, and it is up to each and every one of us to make something of our lives.

"You were right, just now. Your life could have been far worse. All that has happened to you, could have happened in a back street, somewhere in the north of England for instance. And there would have been no money, and no privilege to help you. Nevertheless—" he kissed her cheek "—people come out of that background and most of them fight their way through life, surmounting all difficulties. And you can too. All it needs is guts and determination, and you've got plenty of that as I know to my cost!"

"Oh, Ludo," she gave him a shaky smile. "You're so good for me. I don't know what I would have done without you!"

"You would have done very well, and will do even better in the future. Now, you just lie back and go to sleep."

"Oh, Ludo, please don't leave me," she pleaded fearfully. "Please stay with me...please!"

"Oh Emily..." he sighed. "I must...I really must go back to my own tent. You'll be all right now."

"I won't," she cried. "I know I won't. Oh please. I...." She caught hold of his arm, looking at him beseechingly, feeling terrified at being left alone in the dark night. "I—I just want you to be here, that's all. Nothing else, I—I promise you. Please...."

He looked down at her for a long moment, and then gave a deep sigh. "Very well, Emily. I—I don't seem to be able to refuse you, somehow, although I should. Roll over," he commanded, as he turned to blow out the lamp.

Lying down beside her, he gently drew her into his arms. She sighed, filled with love and comfortable contentment. Snuggled close to him, it was almost possible to dream that she could rest within the safe haven of his arms for all eternity. To feel the strong beat of his heart, to breathe in the warm musky scent of his body, and to be finally released from all doubts and fears.

Ludo lay awake for a long time, his eyes staring blindly into the darkness above their heads. His mouth was clenched in a tight, firm line, the signs of strain on his face deepening as the hours passed. Eventually he fell into a disturbed and fitful sleep, waking every now and then as Emily moved in his arms. The closeness of her warm soft body proving to be every bit as disturbing as he had known it would.

CHAPTER SEVEN

EMILY WOKE AS DAWN CAME to the Ouandan rain forest. The dim light, to which she was becoming accustomed, stealing softly in through the open flap of the tent. Gently turning her head, she looked at the man sleeping beside her. A dark lock of his hair fell over one of his closed eyes, whose lids ended in such long, feathery lashes. She remembered reading in a book how people were supposed to look vulnerable as they slept. Ludo didn't. The skin was stretched firmly over his cheeks, and his mouth was set in a hard line. He looked tough, strong and dangerous as he lay there breathing quietly, and her whole being was suddenly overwhelmed for love of the man she had known for such a short time.

Unable to stop herself, she stretched out her hand and gently slid her fingers through the silver tipped hair at his temples, softly stroking his warm head. She looked down to see that his eyes were open, regarding her steadily and calmly.

"I...er...." She cleared her throat, quickly withdrawing her hand as if she had been burnt.

"Are you feeling better this morning?" he asked in a quiet, expressionless voice, devoid of all the tender feeling that he had shown her last night.

"Yes. I—I'm feeling much better. Thank you for—for being so kind." Blushing furiously, she lay on her back and closed her eyes as a heavy weight of depression seemed to fill her whole being.

"That's good," he said, rolling over to lie half across

her body, looking down at her face only inches from his own.

"You accused me last night of not finding you beautiful," he murmured quietly, his eyes glittering in the dim light. "You know that's not true Emily, don't you?"

She couldn't answer him, as her heart began to thud and pound so loudly that he must be able to hear it, she thought. Breathlessly, she ran her tongue nervously over her dry lips as she recognised the gleaming desire in his eyes.

"I do find you beautiful," he breathed thickly, "so very, very beautiful." His hand trembled as he gently brushed the soft hair from her brow. "But it's no good, my darling. You must see that. One of us has got to have some control over the situation. I . . . ."

Emily reached up to stroke his cheek, her hand moving to lovingly slide through his hair. He trembled at her touch, and she was suddenly swept with such a surge of passion that she couldn't stop herself from drawing his face down towards her trembling, eager lips.

"Don't . . . !" he groaned in agony, as his mouth took possession of her parted lips. Emily's fingers clenched in his hair, as she arched her body closer to his. "Emily . . . oh, Emily! You're driving me insane!" he murmured feverishly, covering her eyes, ears and neck with burning kisses. Her whole being was on fire for him, the blood in her veins a molten stream of white-hot desire. . . .

"No!" Ludo tore his mouth away, and mumbled a savage oath as he wrenched his body from her arms. He rolled away and sat up with his back to her, his powerful chest heaving as he fought for control. "Can't you see . . . ? Can't you see that it's wrong?" He roughly brushed his shaking hands through his hair, his voice sounding harsh and muffled.

"You're in my care, and under my protection," he

ground out through clenched teeth, turning to look at the woman still lying on the ground, her face white with shock. "Oh, my darling, darling Emily," his voice softened. "We mustn't...we really mustn't—ever again. I know I behaved badly, back by the waterfall, and I—I feel such a heel. I should be shot for what I did to you. I...." He shrugged wearily. "I've no excuse—none at all."

Emily couldn't speak; her throat seemed to be constricted, her lungs in the vice of an iron band as she fought to control the shudders which shook her body. She struggled to sit up, placing a soft, beseeching hand on his arm. "But—but I want you make love to me..." she managed to whisper. "Please Ludo. I...I'm not ashamed of that...." Her trembling fingers stroked the hard warmth of his bare shoulders. "I can't see that it's wrong. And—and even if it is wrong, I—I don't care...."

"But I do, my darling. I do," he said quietly with a deep sigh, getting up slowly and leaving the tent with a heavy tread.

Emily lay for a long time staring blindly into space, her body and soul tortured and racked with pain. Again and again, she heard his voice echoing in her ears, and seemed to feel once more the touch of his lips.

There was no way she could face breakfast this morning, she thought. Reluctantly, she began to get dressed, and was grateful to one of the porters who presently brought her a cup of coffee and the long pair of trousers, promised by Ludo the day before.

Dressing slowly in the privacy of the tent, she dismissed all thoughts of how ghastly she must look in the baggy green-and-brown camouflage trousers. Not to mention the bush shirt, she thought with a shrug. Who cared anyway? She certainly didn't, and if she looked like the Michelin man, there was nobody to see, except Ludo.

Emily tried to keep her thoughts firmly off her love for Ludo. It proved to be an impossible task. What a mess they were in—there seemed no way out of the tangle. The moment of bliss as he had kissed her this morning.... You've got to stop thinking about that, she told herself sternly. But I want him, she moaned inwardly; I want him to love me. She lay back on her sleeping bag fighting for control of her emotions.

I ought to be able to handle this in a more sophisticated manner, she thought with despair. What had happened to the cool, calm and collected woman she had once been? That was before she knew what it was to love someone, she told herself sadly. It had been easy to be cold and aloof when she didn't care about anyone else. So easy to be totally disinterested, as she had moved untouched amongst friends and strangers.

She was still trying to find some equilibrium, some calmness, when Ludo coughed outside the tent. "We... er... must go now, Emily. Don't be long."

"I... I'm coming," she croaked hoarsely. "I'll be with you in a minute...."

The journey that day seemed interminable, as they went deeper and deeper into the jungle. Emily, mentally and physically exhausted, just concentrated on putting one foot in front of another as the hours went slowly by. They found another clearing that night, and Emily asked Ludo to go through the medicine chest to see if it contained any sleeping pills. He looked at her steadily, and then left to sort through the case provided by James Martin. Coming back, he silently handed her a bottle, merely saying, "Be careful, Emily. The dose is only one pill. I—I don't want you to have an accident."

"Don't worry Ludo," she snapped bitterly, "You told me to make sure I survived—remember?" She saw him flinch, his face paling at her words. Every fibre of her being cried out with an overwhelming urge to run and put her arms around his neck, and say that she was sorry, she hadn't meant it.... But certain of his rejection, she merely shrugged, turning away to slowly walk back to her lonely tent.

The next day was a repetition of the previous one, except in the mid-afternoon. Ludo had been studying the ground intently. Fetching his binoculars, he took her hand, putting a finger to his lips, signalling silence. He gestured to the porters to wait, as he walked slowly and quietly to the edge of a clearing.

Motioning to Emily to squat down in the under-growth, he joined her, putting the binoculars to his eyes as he scanned the peaceful scene in front of them. "Ah..." he breathed in satisfaction, passing her the glasses and pointing to the right. Emily couldn't see anything for a moment, and then gave a gasp as she saw a large gorilla sitting in what looked like a nest of eucalyptus leaves.

She'd only seen such a creature on television, and so was surprised and awed by the sheer size of the animal. His huge face looked almost comically content as he chewed on a large shoot, occasionally scratching his dark fur. Presently he got up, moving on all fours over to a group of slightly smaller gorillas, which included some babies. The hair on the large male gorilla's back was silver. As he stood up for a moment, to pluck a particularly succulent leaf, she thought he must be well over six feet.

"Oh, look at the baby—isn't it sweet," she whispered, watching a mother groom and tidy her infant. Reluctantly, she passed the glasses back to Ludo, who smiled warmly at her and continued his observation.

"We'll have to go," he said at last. "I'm glad you saw them. That male is a particularly good specimen. Back to the route march, I'm afraid."

"Thank you for showing them to me, Ludo." Her

eyes shone with pleasure. "They all seemed to be sitting in some sort of 'nest' if that's the right word."

"Yes, it is," he replied, as they made their way back to rejoin the porters. "They make a fresh nest every day. Very clean and hygienic is the gorilla!"

They resumed their progress, stopping for a short break an hour later. Emily wandered restlessly around the clearing, almost absent-mindedly picking some trailing vines and orchids.

The high-pitched chatter of a porter, as he called to Emily, alerted Ludo to the danger. He jumped up and sped over to her, dashing the flowers and vines from her hands with a heavy blow.

"Ludo!" Emily staggered back, reeling with shock from his violence, her face suddenly ashen with fright.

"Let me see your hands," he commanded, his voice stern and angry. She looked at him uncomprehendingly as he seized her elbow, turning her arm towards him and looking intently at her skin. "I thought so," he shouted. "You stupid girl!"

"I...what...?" Emily looked at his angry face in astonishment, and then at the red weals of the rash on her arm. "I—I didn't...."

"You didn't think—I know. Do I ever know!" He dragged her off towards the medicine chest. "I just hope James has given us some stuff," he said through clenched teeth. "Of all the stupid things to do—you silly girl!"

"You—you mean the plants were poisonous?" she asked in dazed amazement, her numbed hands beginning to sting from his blow. "You never said...."

"I can't be expected to tell you everything, can I? God preserve me from fools." Ludo was still very angry.

"If you didn't tell me, how in the hell was I to know?" she cried. Her hands ached and the rash was beginning to feel prickly and sore.

"Anyone with any sense would have known not to touch strange plants. But not you—oh, no!" He was shaking with suppressed fury as he rubbed ointment on the rash.

"You really are a foul man! If my hands weren't so sore, I'd—I'd slap your beastly face. There's no need to be so bloody-minded—none at all. It's a mistake anyone could make!" she shouted angrily, fighting to control her tears.

This row wasn't about her mistake in picking poisonous plants, and they both knew it, she thought tearfully. Inexperienced as she was, even she could see that in trying to control his passionate need for her, Ludo was placing an intolerable strain on them both. Having to be in each other's company, day in and day out, was becoming more than she, at least, could bear.

"Don't be so angry with me. Please, Ludo," she whispered as he spread ointment on her arm. "It's—it's not fair of you," she added with a sniff, turning her head to try and wipe away on the shoulder of her shirt, the tears which she couldn't stop from falling.

The cords of Ludo's neck were strained and a muscle beat wildly in his clenched jaw. He sighed heavily, his hands gradually becoming more gentle. "There, I'm done. You should be all right now. I. . . ." He put an arm about her trembling figure, drawing her gently against his hard chest. "I'm sorry, Emily. It . . . er . . . somehow it's been a long trip. With any luck we'll be out of the rain forest tomorrow. I. . . I'm sorry. It's been a strain for both of us, hasn't it?" He kissed her eyes, wet with tears, before reluctantly letting her go.

They made rapid progress the next day as the rain forest proper began to give way to more and more deciduous trees. They carefully skirted many deserted villages, some of which showed signs of having been bombed and strafed by aeroplanes. Of the inhabitants, who had fled their homes, there was no sign.

About noon, they came upon a larger village. Ludo venturing on a careful reconnaissance, found a rusty Jeep and some petrol in a lean-to shed. "Our transport problem has been solved," he announced, and proceeded to confer with the porters in what Emily had come to understand was the Bantu language.

"The porters have decided to stay here for a bit, and rest up before they return," he told her as they ate their midday meal. "Apparently there is quite a good store of food, and as it's a Bantu village they have no fear of trouble when the villagers return. We'll just finish eating and load up. It won't be long before we're on our way."

Emily knew she ought to be thankful that they had left the rain forest, and that the end of their journey was in sight. Yet she felt overwhelmingly depressed at the realisation of just how little time they had left together. With a heavy heart she helped to put their things into the Jeep, and after saying goodbye to the porters, they proceeded on their way.

"I'm not expecting any more trouble," said Ludo, as they wound their way down a dirt track. "The nearer we get to the Cameroon, the less likelihood of aeroplanes bothering us. The Ouandan forces won't want to tangle with the Cameroon army, not if they can help it."

Ludo proved to be right. They had a trouble-free run for the rest of the day, climbing higher on to the wide plains, leaving the forest valley far behind them. The sun was just beginning to set, when Ludo halted their vehicle and turned smiling to Emily.

"Miss Lambouchere—I presume...?" he paused, and then continued with a grin, "I presume you realise that for the last hour we have been in the Cameroon. I wasn't entirely sure at first, but now the matter is beyond doubt." He pointed to a sign. République Unie du Cameroon, Département de Boumba—Ngoko.

"We'll just go on for a bit and find somewhere to camp for the night." He glanced sideways at Emily's set face. "You don't seem very happy about it?" he said, with a frown. "Are you feeling all right?"

"I'm fine," she answered in a dull voice. "What happens now, Ludo? I—I haven't really thought about it. I mean, so okay we're in the Cameroon, so where do we go now?"

"I have some friends who don't live too far away. Marc and Julie Roget have been living out here for some time. He works for L'institut français d'Afrique noir, specialising in sociology and ethnology. In fact," he explained, "he doesn't have to work for them; he's very wealthy in his own right. However, he's engaged on a study of the Bantu people. I'm sure you'll like them."

They stopped and made camp by a small stream for the last time. Ludo went off to have a wash before supper, leaving Emily feeling unbearably sad as she realised that this would be the last night she and Ludo would spend alone...alone in the open together. She tried valiantly to make an effort, but even she thought her voice sounded hollow as they sat talking idly by the fire after their meal—a meal she had hardly been able to eat.

Suddenly, her tortured feelings grew too much for her to cope with and she made a hurried excuse. She fled to the Jeep, grabbing her case and making for a small group of trees by the stream. The moonlight was very bright, and she could see that the water was a bit muddy and, she suspected, none too clean. However, the blessed relief of being able to wash herself all over was enormous. They had had to husband their precious water so carefully during the trip, that to splash and roll in the water was a luxury beyond belief.

She stepped out and dried herself on her towel, smiling wryly as she remembered the fuss she had made on her first night camping out with Ludo. No wonder he had looked amazed at her silk nightgown—what a fool she had been! That nightgown had been lost days ago on their travels, and she now wrapped herself sarong style in her damp towel, going over to sit on a smooth rock by the stream.

If only...if only...if only...the words beat a tattoo in her brain. If only Ludo hadn't been married to a jet-set wife...if only Emily wasn't the sole survivor of the rich Lambouchere family...if only he could love her as she loved him.... The "if onlys" were legion! It seemed as if, after tomorrow, they would part, and the chances of their meeting again were so slim as to be minimal. After so many achingly long years of loneliness, to find a man at last, a man who had come to mean so much, and then to lose him again. Emily clasped her arms about her knees in agony.

She was alerted to Ludo's presence by the smell of his cigar smoke. She looked up quickly, to see him standing a few feet away, silently watching her. How— how long had he been standing there? For the first time she noticed that the lines on either side of his wide, mobile mouth had become deeply etched. She was unable to take her eyes from his face, her heart filled with bitterness and pain as they gazed intently at each other.

Ludo broke the silence. "Did you enjoy your wash?" he asked her. "The water looks a little muddy."

She tore her eyes away from the face she loved so much and looked blindly at the small stream. "Yes, it was marvellous," Emily murmured. Why are we talking such banalities, she wanted to scream. Instead of which, she rose, and picked up her case. "I'll leave you to smoke in peace," she muttered, picking her way over the stones towards him. He stepped back to let her go by. Noticing his movement of withdrawal she gasped, feeling as if he had driven a knife of cold steel into her heart, and suddenly it felt as if something seemed to snap inside her head.

"I haven't got the plague, you know! I'm not exactly contagious!" she screamed, throwing her case at him as hard as she could, and running away to fall weeping in the long grass by the Jeep. She was racked by deep, painful sobs which shook her body so fiercely that she was certain she'd never be able to stop, when she felt Ludo's strong arms close about her. Picking her up as lightly as if she was thistledown, he held her cradled in his embrace, carrying her over to the fire.

"Ludo...I...." She shivered as he laid her gently down on the sleeping-bags he had placed by the warmth of the smouldering logs. The evening air was becoming chilly, as he had forecast, and she trembled, both from the cold and the look in his eyes, as he sat down beside her.

"I'm—I'm sorry." Emily touched his arm with innocent provocation. Her ash-blond hair formed an aureole around her head, the soft curls tumbling about her shoulders. "I've tried...tried so hard..." she murmured softly, fluttering her eyelashes which still held tiny droplets of the tears she had shed in the grass. She was unknowingly entrancing, as with trembling lips she looked at him in sorrow.

"I know," he said thickly, "we both have...." He cleared his throat. "Emily, don't look at me that way!"

Emily's lips parted. "Ludo..." she whispered huskily, feeling the muscles of his arm tense under her fingers, noticing that a pulse was beating wildly at his temple.

"Don't tempt me, Emily!" he cried in anguish, looking down at her with tortured eyes. His face was taut with emotion, and unable to help herself, she lifted a hand and laid it gently on his cheek.

His strong fingers captured hers and held them tightly for a moment as he gazed at her wide blue eyes, darkening with desire. Her bare shoulders gleamed in the firelight as they rose above the loosely tied towel, slack enough to display the rising fullness of her warm, creamy breasts.

With a groan, he bent his head and kissed the soft skin of her shoulder. At the touch of his lips, she shuddered uncontrollably, tremors of delight dancing across her skin as his mouth moved lower. Almost unable to help himself and with the utmost gentleness, Ludo undid her towel, his hands trembling as he slowly pushed the material aside, exposing her fully to his view.

His powerful body shook with tension as he tried to control his mounting passion. "I—I want you, Emily...and so help me...I think I've got to take you!" he groaned thickly, burying his face in her soft breasts.

Emily's breathing quickened, and totally beyond her control, her body moved sensually and invitingly beneath him. Her urgent fingers sought to undo the buttons of his shirt, Ludo's strong body shaking as he felt her soft hands moving over the curly hair of his chest. Her fingers probed lower and unable to contain himself any longer, he swiftly divested himself of his clothes, before seizing her lovely body to his and covering it with kisses.

The relief, the inexpressible joy of being able at last to express her love for the man who meant everything in life to her, was so great that Emily cried out in rapture as the sensuous and erotic caresses of his skillful fingers banished all thoughts of right and wrong. Their bodies melted together as they yielded to the overwhelmingly urgent excitement that filled them both.

Emily revelled in the firmness of his body, the hard muscles of his thighs, the strength of his arms about her. She had never felt more vibrantly alive as the cool night air gently fanned their fevered bodies, and they became as one in an ecstatic peak of emotional frenzy.

It was light when they awoke, the fresh dawn air moistening their limbs as they lay entwined. Emily opened her eyes to see Ludo gazing at her with a warm and tender gaze. He ran his hands caressingly over her supple body. "Emily Lambouchere, what a wonderful girl you are!"

"You—you don't regret...you aren't sorry...?" she whispered.

"Darling girl—it's far too late to worry about that. I—I wanted you so badly..." he sighed. "I wanted you more than any other woman I've ever known. But you knew that, surely?"

"Well...yes..." she murmured. "But you were so tough and fierce, that I gave up any hope of you losing your iron control!" She peeped at him through her long eyelashes, as she trailed her fingers over his long, brown legs.

"What are you up to?" he smiled, as she leant over him, her warm soft hands caressing his body.

"You, I hope!" she whispered, bending down to kiss his firm lips.

"Em-i-ly!" His husky laugh was warm and tender, as he firmly held her waist. "What a baggage you are!" he muttered, their kiss deepening as his fingers came up to clasp the warm, firm breasts poised so invitingly above him. "Seriously, my darling," he said breathlessly as he rolled her over. "We ought to start clearing up and get on the road." He looked down into the blue eyes smiling lazily and languuorously up at him, and knew that he was lost.

"To hell with it!" he groaned, his voice thick with passionate desire. His hands and mouth roamed over her body before his lips caught and held the swollen rosy tip of her breast.

As the mastery of his lovemaking overwhelmed her,

Emily's last coherent thought was of how much she loved him, as she slowly slipped beneath the waves of pulsating, ecstatic excitement that he was always able to invoke in her. Far above their heads, the eagles wheeled and soared as their two bodies became one under the fresh morning light of an African dawn.

THE JEEP BOWLED ALONG the tarmac road, so very different to the dirt tracks that they had been on for the past days. Emily looked at the scenery with interest, her glowing eyes and luminous skin lighting up the interior of the Jeep. Earlier on, there had been a problem as Ludo, realising that they needed more petrol, cursed the fact that unlike his Land Rover, the Jeep carried no spare cans of fuel.

"We'll have to stop at a garage soon, and the one thing we haven't got between us, is any hard currency," he said with annoyance.

Emily looked at him for a moment and then smiled. "We may not have any 'coin of the realm,'" she said, "but I'll get you some petrol just the same!"

"Be practical, Emily," he said firmly, and then sighed. "Oh, well, I can always demand it at the point of a rifle, I suppose. Not ideal, but I can sort out the mess later."

"Oh, ye of little faith!'" she giggled. Emily had been in irrepressible spirits following their lovemaking and felt, indeed she knew, that there wasn't anything she couldn't accomplish with Ludo by her side. Kneeling up, she leant back over the seat, sorting through the boxes and cases they brought with them. She opened and shut a case, and then sat down smiling again.

"Just leave this to me, Ludo," she said as they drove into the dusty forecourt of a tumbledown garage. "Give me ten minutes—Okay?"

Ludo shrugged as she opened the door and stepped down. Looking extraordinarily elegant, despite her shorts and shirt, Emily strolled into the dark interior of the little office. A few minutes later, far less than the time she had asked for, two Africans ran out. One grabbed the pumps while the other began to frantically polish the windscreen.

He watched astonished as Emily, grinning at him in the strong sunlight, commanded the Africans, in excellent French, to hose down the vehicle as well, before she disappeared into the office again. A moment later she climbed back into the Jeep and lay laughing against the seat. *"Allez-vous-en, mon brave!"* she gasped when she could catch her breath. "Oh, Ludo, if you could see your face!"

"How in the world did you do it?" He smiled at her as they drove on down the road.

"We didn't have any money—right? What else did I have, that you created such a fuss about back at the mine, when we had to leave in such a hurry?" she grinned.

"Oh, Emily! Your jewellery—you didn't...you couldn't have!" He looked at her sternly.

"For heaven's sake, Ludo! Who cares about a trumpery piece of jewellery when we couldn't go anywhere without petrol?" She looked at him, the smile draining from her face as she saw his hard frowning expression. "Darling, I—I have changed since we began our journey. You've helped to teach me the true values of life. You know you have," she said softly. "I was merely putting my new philosophy into practice."

"It's still wrong. You shouldn't have done it."

"Ludo, please be sensible. It was a small diamond brooch that I've never particularly liked, which some old aunt left me. It wasn't," she said almost tearfully, as his stern face looked at her unrelenting, "it wasn't as if it had enormous sentimental value. You must see," she pleaded looking anxiously at his hard, frosty grey eyes and the firm tight line of his mouth, "that I'm one of the few people who *can* give away diamonds, and not miss them. Surely you can see that?''

"Yes,'' he said grimly. "We had managed to forget about that for a while, hadn't we?'' He sighed, leaning over to give her a peck on the cheek. "It was a clever thought, Emily, and I'm sorry if I appeared to be crabby.''

"That's all right then,'' she said happily, pulling two chocolate bars out of her shirt pocket. "These got thrown in for good measure. I should hate to think you were too proud to enjoy a piece,'' she grinned, popping some into his mouth.

"You are an incorrigible girl, Emily! But thank you, it's delicious,'' he said with a sideways grin. However, looking at her later, as she sat glowing with happiness beside him, his eyes became clouded. It seemed cruel to prick her bubble of euphoria, but.... He shrugged; time enough for that later on.

"How far have we to go, Ludo?'' Emily's voice cut into his thoughts.

"Not far—we should be there very soon. I asked James Martin to get a call through to Marc Roget, on the transmitter in my Land Rover. So they should be expecting us, even if they don't know the exact time and day.'' And it was only half an hour later when they turned off the road, and drove down a long drive, towards a large group of trees surrounding a sprawling bungalow.

As they drew up, dogs ran out barking, rapidly followed by what seemed a steady stream of children calling *"Oncle Ludo, Oncle Ludo,"* and leaping on him with great excitement. He stood up, holding the youngest in his arms, smiling over at the couple who had come out on to the porch of the bungalow.

Emily, suddenly feeling shy, stood quietly by the Jeep as Ludo was welcomed by Marc and Julie Roget.

Marc was almost as tall as Ludo, his fair hair bleached white by the sun, in sharp contrast to his wife, who was small, dark and petite.

As soon as she saw Emily, Julie ran over to take her hands in welcome, her brown eyes shining with friendliness. "Welcome, welcome," she said in French. "We are so pleased and relieved that you are safe and well."

Emily felt instantly drawn to Julie, and smiled back with relief. She had been dreading having to meet Ludo's friends, who might have been as antagonistic towards her, as he himself had originally been, when they first met at the mine.

Julie led her into the cool interior of the bungalow, chattering very fast and asking innumerable questions. "Please Madame Roget...please, not so fast," Emily laughed. "My French isn't too bad, but I'm out of practice."

"Julie," the dark girl laughed. "You must call me Julie...and you are Emily? Good. I will try to speak slower, but as Marc will tell you—it is an impossible task!" she laughed again as the men joined them.

"I do not know about you, Ludo," she said, "but I am absolutely sure that Emily here will want a bath—immediately!"

"Oh, yes," Emily groaned with pleasure. "What a fantastic idea!"

"That's taken care of that," Julie smiled. "Marc, you look after Ludo, will you? I expect he would like a shower and a cool beer. Have you anything you want from the Jeep, Emily?" she asked.

"Not a damn thing! I never, never want to see any of those clothes, as long as I live!" Emily laughed, following Julie along a corridor. "It really is very kind of you, to allow us to invade your home like this," she said.

"Absolutely not. Ludo is a very special friend. There is—well, there is nothing that Marc and I would not do for him. Here you are." She ushered Emily into a large bathroom containing a sunken bath in the middle of the floor.

"My goodness," gasped Emily, thinking that she had never seen a more welcome sight.

Julie shrugged. "One has to take many baths in this climate, so it seems sensible to make them as comfortable as possible...*n'est-ce pas*?"

"Oh I agree," Emily said fervently. "Thank you so much, Julie. I—I'm so grateful."

"You are a nice girl, Emily," Julie reached up and planted a kiss on the tall girl's cheek. "Now you have a long, long bath and then a good sleep. Take just as long as you want. I will go and see if I can find some clothes for you."

Left alone, Emily started to run the bath water, hurriedly and thankfully stripping off the clothes she had worn for so long. Stepping into the rose-scented water, thick with bubbles from the lotion Julie had provided, she sighed with pleasure.

Nothing in her life could approach the joy of Ludo's lovemaking, but this bath...well, after their epic journey, it came very close....

CHAPTER EIGHT

EMILY WAS DREAMING. Not the nightmare which had haunted so much of her life, but a happy joyous dream where she and Ludo were wandering through fields of flowers. He turned to touch her shoulder, and began to shake it harder and harder.... Emily opened her eyes to see Julie bending over her.

"I have brought up a cup of your English tea," Julie said, with a faint smile. "I wasn't sure whether to wake you," she added hesitantly.

"Oh, my goodness." Emily sat up, rubbing her eyes and looking out of the window at the setting sun. "I must have slept for hours."

"Only a short time," Julie said, smiling as she passed Emily a cup and sitting down on the end of the bed.

Emily smiled lazily at the dark woman. "I feel really great—absolutely marvellous. First the bath and then a sleep—on sheets for heaven's sake—such luxury! You've no idea," she confided with a smile, "how I've longed to lie on cool, clean sheets. It's really amazing how one takes the good things of life for granted. I hope and pray I never do so again."

"Yes, you are lucky to be alive." Julie looked seriously at her guest. "There has been so much bloodshed," she said, shuddering. "We could hear nothing from Ouanda for a long time, all our news coming from Zaire or the BBC Overseas Service. We were so worried when we heard that Ludo had disappeared."

"I know I'm lucky," Emily said earnestly. "I...well,

I wouldn't have survived without Ludo's help, never in a million years. I can't say I appreciated it all at the time...not at the beginning, anyway. I was awful, really awful," she said, slowly. "The absolute epitome of a spoilt brat. That's what Ludo called me, and he was right!"

"But, my dear Emily, you do not strike me like that. No, not at all," Julie smiled at the beautiful woman, as she sat up in bed drinking her tea.

"Oh I was, I really was," Emily earnestly assured her. "You've no idea how foul and horrid I was. When he made me change the wheel of the Land Rover, I—I nearly brained him with the jack!" She lay back on the pillows, laughing weakly. "We had some terrible fights, we really did."

"But Ludo seems very fond of you."

"I—I hope so...." Emily blushed under the dark woman's quizzical look. "I—I do care for him, very—very much indeed," she said simply, her eyes shining with tender love as she recollected how much they had gone through together.

Julie looked at the woman sitting in the bed, her whole being glowing with adoration for the man who had rescued her. She couldn't possibly tell Emily of the arrangements she had heard discussed between Ludo and Marc, as she had served them with a cool drink before coming along to see Emily. She ached with pity for the beautiful woman and sought to change the subject into safer channels.

"I must go and prepare supper," she said, getting up. "There is the baby to be fed as well. A woman's work is never done," she laughed. "Now, I have put some clothes out for you, which if not in the forefront of fashion will, I hope, be a change from your shorts and blouse. Is there anything else I can get you?"

"You've been so thoughtful, Julie. I'll never be able

to repay your kindness." Emily beamed at the French girl. "Proper clothes—at last! I can hardly believe it."

Oh, the bliss, the sheer bliss of putting on clean clothes that didn't smell of river water—or worse—thought Emily, fastening the white skirt about her waist. Normally very slim, she noticed that she had lost some weight during their journey, and was thus able to get into Julie's clothes without too much difficulty. She was still without a bra, alas; there was no way that the French girl's measurements came near to her own. That's the next bit of luxury, she promised herself, a bra that really fits.

In the meantime she was not dissatisfied, as she looked in the full-length mirror. She had become so used to her curly hair that she no longer worried about it. Ludo had said how much he liked it, so she would probably leave it to grow in future as nature had intended that it should.

The scooped-neck, sleeveless white blouse was a little tight, but beggars can't be choosers, she reminded herself wryly, and the flared white cotton skirt, while admittedly very short, fitted her waist and hips like a glove. Easing her feet into a pair of Indian leather flip-flops, she left the room to find Julie.

Wondering whether to go left or right of the broad corridor in which she found herself, she heard her hostess' voice coming from a room a few doors away. Putting her head around the open door, she found Julie sprinkling talcum powder on a baby's bottom before doing up the nappy.

"Come in." Julie's words were muffled and indistinct because of the nappy pins in her mouth. "There, that's better," she said as she finished and held the baby up in her arms. "Phillipe—meet Emily!"

"How do you do, Phillipe." Emily grinned and walked over, taking hold of the baby's little hands. "Oh do look," she breathed in wonder, "his fingers curl into his hand like a little starfish. Isn't—isn't he lovely!"

"He's a little devil at times—but that's men for you!" Julie placed the baby in Emily's arms. Savouring his smell of soap and talcum powder, she bent her head to kiss him gently as he snuggled into her shoulder.

"I...I've never held a baby before...." She looked with shining eyes at Julie. "He's sweet, so cuddly." She bent down to place her cheek against his. Phillipe gurgled and smiled before reaching out and grabbing one of her curls. "Ow!" she moaned, as he tugged hard.

"See what I mean!" Julie laughed. "Still, I would be very grateful if you could give him his bottle. I've got behind hand with dinner, and it would help me to catch up—if you don't mind?"

"Mind? Of course I don't mind. However, I've never done anything like that before, so you'd better give me a teach-in Julie. I'd hate to do something wrong."

After the necessary instructions, Julie went off to see to her cooking, and Emily was left to feed Phillipe. "I hope you know what you're doing, Master Phillipe, because I haven't a clue," she smiled happily down at the baby. Phillipe indeed knew exactly what to do, snatching at the teat and beginning to chomp away happily.

Half-way through, mindful of Julie's advice, she removed the bottle from Phillipe who protested lustily, which frightened her for a moment. However, she had to sit him up and burp him, as she explained to the baby who was looking at her with accusatory eyes.

Gingerly she sat him up, placing a hand on his tummy to support him while she gently rubbed his back. "I ought to sing you a lullaby," she told him, "but it will have to be in French, and I don't think...oh, yes I do," she laughed softly. Every English child must have been brought up on it, she thought, as she softly began to sing, *"Frère Jacques, frère Jacques, dormez-vous...."*

Standing silently in the doorway, Ludo watched as Emily sang softly to the baby cradled in her arms. Her head was bent forward, hiding her face and exposing her neck which made her look oddly defenceless and vulnerable. The baby gave a large burp, and laughing, Emily held him up before her.

"Oh, you beautiful, clever boy, Phillipe," she said, turning to see Ludo standing in the doorway. "Isn't he lovely," she smiled radiantly at him. "Isn't he a fantastic baby?"

Emily felt her happy smile slipping as Ludo stood silently facing her, an expression in his eyes that she found hard to define. It had been a long trip for him, she thought suddenly, looking at the weary slump of his shoulders. He'd had all the trouble of looking after her, as well as having to do the driving and plan their escape. She longed to run into his arms and smooth the frown from between his eyes.

"There's a drink ready for you, when you've finished feeding the baby," he said abruptly, before turning away.

Confused, Emily looked at the empty doorway. Surely it couldn't be that he didn't like babies? No, it wasn't that—he'd been laughing and teasing the Roget children as they'd entered the house on their arrival. It must be... it must be that he's tired and exhausted, she thought, trying to dismiss an uneasy feeling in the pit of her stomach.

Julie returned to find Phillipe sound asleep in Emily's arms, a small trickle of milk oozing from his mouth, which was smiling contentedly. "You're so lucky," Emily whispered, as she handed the sleeping baby back to his mother. "He's adorable."

"Can I help you with the cooking, Julie?" she said following the French woman to the kitchen.

"Are you a good cook, Emily?" Julie asked with interest, as she tied an apron around her waist.

"Well...er...no. In fact," she confessed, "I don't even know how to boil an egg, which is supposed to be one of the easiest things to do, I believe!"

"Really?" Julie looked at her in amazement.

"Really," Emily confirmed, with a shameful grin. "Is it very hard to learn? I mean—will it take me a long time? I...I've decided that it is of supreme importance that I learn—fast." She looked down at her feet trying to hide the tell-tale blush she could feel sweeping over her face.

"It—it sounds so stupid to say that I've always had servants to do that sort of thing, Julie; but it's true. I'm really ashamed of how little I know about real life, and—and I do want to learn."

"Wanting to learn is all that is important, Emily," the dark woman said evenly. "When you return to England, why don't you enrol for a cordon bleu course in cookery? That is surely one way to learn well, and fast!" she smiled encouragingly.

"In the meantime, go through and have a drink with Marc and Ludo. I will finish the cooking, and sometime in the future I will come and have a meal with you, when you can do the cooking."

"It's a bargain," laughed Emily, "although I will arrange to have a doctor standing by, just in case!"

"Hello, you two," said Emily, as she came into the main room of the sprawling bungalow, where Marc and Ludo were sitting and talking quietly. "I've been banished from the kitchen—fortunately for you all—and am hoping to be offered a drink."

The men had risen at her entrance, Marc looking with started bemusement at a woman he would never have recognised from the one he had met earlier in the day. That woman had been travel-stained and weary, her face streaked with the dust of the road, while this woman—this woman was ravishing!

He gazed open mouthed at the clean, shining mass of ash-blond curls, the low-cut blouse which drew attention to her magnificent bosom, and the long, long slim brown legs beneath the short skirt. Involuntarily he put up a hand to adjust a non-existent tie, before catching the sardonic gleam in Ludo's eyes as he watched Marc fall a victim to Emily's beauty.

"You may be a fool, Ludo, but I'm certainly not!" he murmured, before leaping forward to welcome Emily, and to ask what she would like to drink. Placing a glass in her hand, he put his arm about her waist and ushered her out into the garden, glancing triumphantly back at Ludo who followed his progress with a slight frown.

The children were splashing in the pool, and they watched for a moment as Marc's eldest son, a boy of ten, dived off a small low board into the water. "I've just met Phillipe," she said with a smile. "He's a really lovely baby. Are these all yours?" she asked, gesturing to the three children in the pool.

"Yes—alas! However, I will discard them immediately, if you will promise to run away with me tonight, you beautiful creature." Marc grinned, raising her hand to his lips.

"Do you know," Emily said, smiling, "I had forgotten just how charming Frenchmen can be. Now I know I'm back in civilization! Julie," she called, as his wife came out to join them by the pool. "Your husband has just offered to run off with me—do you think I should accept?" she asked with a laugh. "I'm quite tempted, really...."

"Oh, do!" urged Julie, laughing at Marc's shamefaced grin, and secure in the knowledge of where Emily's heart lay. "Really, Emily, I've been trying to get rid of him for ages, but alas—it's so tragic—no one will have him!"

The women collapsed into laughter as Marc sighed. "The female mafia—there's no way a man can win! I think we all need another drink. Come on kids, time for bed," he called to his children as he walked back to the house.

Julie's dinner, cooked to perfection, was delicious. "Wonderful, wonderful food," Emily sighed happily, as they sat with their coffee and brandy around the dark mahogany table.

"You never said that when you ate my cooking." Ludo who had been rather silent at dinner, grinned across the table at her.

"Oh come on!" laughed Emily. "You told me you were no Escoffier—and how right you were. Honestly," she confided to Marc and Julie, "I thought that if I saw another plateful of baked beans—I'd die!"

"Well, baked beans or no—you escaped," Marc spoke seriously. "And that's more than can be said of many hundreds of people in Ouanda."

"I know," Emily felt instantly contrite. "I—I feel so awful really. When I think of those poor people at the mine...." She sighed deeply. 'What's going to happen to the country?"

"Well," said Marc, "it's a case of what's happened already I suppose. Two days ago the French flew in a considerable number of paratroopers, as I believe Ludo here forecast that they would. They seem to have captured the key installations, and General Ngaro has fled the country. It appears that the French are supporting Edovard Dolle, a right of centre moderate figure, for president. It looks as if he will be acceptable to most of the tribes."

"What about the mercenaries?" she asked.

"From all we can gather," Marc replied, "their numbers have been drastically reduced since they seemed to have spent most of their time fighting each other. Those that are left, are being rounded up by the French.''

''That was something interesting,'' Ludo turned to Marc. ''You remember Mad Mike Clifton...?''

''Do I not!'' said Marc, with feeling.

''Well, Emily and I had him in our rifle sights at one point. It was by the waterfall,'' he explained to Emily.

''You should have killed him while you had the chance.'' Marc's voice grated sharply.

Emily looked at the Frenchman in surprise. ''Why—what has he done? Apart from being a mercenary, of course.''

''His nickname was the Butcher of Stanleyville,'' Julie answered slowly. ''He was a mercenary in the Congo, and—and he shot and killed my parents—just for kicks—amongst the other hundreds of people he's killed in his time.''

''Oh, Julie...I'm so sorry,'' Emily looked at her, feeling overcome with compassion. ''Why didn't we kill him?'' she turned angrily to Ludo. ''I could have got him, plumb in the middle, easily.''

''My darling, blood-thirsty girl! His troops were carrying howitzers—that's why. One stray shot from us, and in return he'd have made sure there was nothing left of us! Emily's a great shot,'' he assured his friends, ''but it was too risky. I'm sorry Julie. I know you'll believe me when I tell you that I was sorely tempted.''

''I know, Ludo,'' she said, smiling gently at him. ''He will get his just desserts, never fear.''

''What puzzles me,'' Marc said with a frown, ''is why General Ngaro or his mercenary troops bothered with the mine. Why didn't they just nationalise it like they have with so many other concerns?''

''Because of de Beers,'' Emily replied absently, handing her cup to Julie for more coffee.

"But they don't own the mine, do they? What have they to do with it?"

"They control the distribution of all diamonds throughout the world," Emily explained. "Really, it was practically the only sensible thing my father ever did. He never wanted anything to do with his inheritance—except to live shut away from the world. So he made a deal with de Beers, whereby they not only distribute the diamonds, but also advise in the management of the mine—for a 'slice of the action' of course." Marc still looked puzzled, so she explained further.

"General Ngaro—or whoever—could grab the mine, but without de Beers he can't sell his diamonds. All diamonds are sold through de Beers—or they aren't sold at all! Since they also have an interest in how the mine is run, he would have been very foolish to try and nationalise it. He'd be stuck with diamonds nobody would buy. The mine produces mostly industrial diamonds, and since General Ngaro got a hefty wack of the profits in tax every year, I don't know why there was any trouble there in the first place."

"Everything just got out of control." Ludo stood up. "Once you bring in a strange army it's very difficult to control them, very difficult indeed." He stretched. "It's a lovely night, and I'm going for a walk in the garden. Come and join me, Emily."

"Yes, I'd love to. Thank you for the delicious meal, Julie." She leant over and kissed her new friend's cheek. "I'll never be able to cook like that—but I'll have fun and grow fat trying to!" With a smile she got up from the table and went to join Ludo by the door to the garden.

Left on their own, Julie and Marc looked at each other unhappily for some moments. Eventually Julie stood up and began to stack the plates. "He is one big fool," she murmured sadly, making her way to the kitchen.

"It's lovely out here in the moonlight," Emily sighed contentedly, putting her arm through Ludo's. "Julie and Marc have been so kind, and so generous. What are we going to do tomorrow?" she asked, surprised at how silent Ludo was being.

"I'm taking you to the airport at Yaoundé, Emily," he said in a bland voice.

"And where are we flying to?" she asked with a smile.

"We aren't. You are flying to London, alone."

"But—what do you mean? Do you mean you aren't coming with me? Oh why Ludo? There's no need to take separate flights, surely."

"Emily." His voice was suddenly hard and stern. "There's no way I can ever go with you. Now or in the future. You must go back to your own life, your own environment."

"I—I don't understand what you're saying...." Emily looked at him with dazed eyes, the vague apprehension she had felt all evening beginning to tighten into a horrific and unbelievable reality.

"You—you mean you're intending to put me on an aeroplane tomorrow and—and never see me again? Is that what you're saying, Ludo?"

"That's exactly what I'm saying, Emily." His tone was harsh and strained in the still night.

"But—but you can't!" she cried. "Not after—after everything! Oh, Ludo, please—please don't do this to me...."

Ludo sighed heavily, taking her hand and leading her gently over to a stone bench set under a tree in the moonlit garden.

"My darling Emily," he said quietly, taking both her hands in his. "I think you're a marvellous, wonderful girl. You have my full and wholehearted admiration, both for your stamina and courage. I can think of few people, let alone a girl of your age, who would have survived our trip with such fortitude. I did tell you that you were a born survivor, didn't I?"

He gave a low, rueful laugh. "You have my word of honour that I will never, ever again, accuse you of being a silly little rich girl. You have proved that you are capable of surmounting the toughest obstacles, and I want you to know that I'm very proud of you indeed."

"Thank—thank you, Ludo. But...."

"Hush, my darling girl. Let me finish what I have to say. We...er...we were thrown closely together during our trip, weren't we? There can be no doubt that I..." he sighed. "Well, I proved to be a weak man, completely unable to resist the overwhelming urge and temptation to make love to you."

"But—but I wanted you to, Ludo. You know I did," she cried urgently.

"I know. We both...er...." He shrugged unhappily. "I can't defend my actions. I have no excuse for my behaviour—none at all!" he grated harshly in the darkness.

Emily couldn't stop herself from shivering with fear and tension. "Ludo! You mustn't blame yourself. It wasn't like that!"

"Oh, yes, Emily, it was exactly like that!" He gripped her hands tightly, his hard grey eyes staring intently into hers. "Emily, you must understand what has happened to you. Suddenly, without any warning, you found yourself in an alien world and thrown into close proximity with a man you...er...you found attractive. My darling, we both know that you hadn't had any previous sexual experience. Not to put too fine a point upon it—and to my eternal shame—you were a virgin." His voice was low and bitterly self-accusatory.

"My—my virginity isn't important..." Emily cried in anguish. "I—I love you. I love you with all my heart. Please, Ludo...I've no pride left...I just want to live with you and look after you, and—and love you for the rest of my life." She blinked furiously as she felt tears welling up in her eyes.

"My sweet Emily," he murmured softly. "Of course you think you're in love with me. I'm the first man to have made love to you, and you also know that I care about you. Of course you think that you've fallen in love with me—it's perfectly natural that you should."

He let go of her hands, placing an arm about her trembling shoulders. "But my darling one, what you feel for me isn't really love—you must see that. You will fall in and out of love many times before you find the right man."

"You're wrong...you're so wrong," she cried impatiently, certain that she must be in the midst of a living nightmare. "I'm not a silly little girl any more. I *know* I love you—I really do!"

"My dear," he sighed deeply, cupping her face in his strong, brown hands. "You don't know what you're talking about. You're just a child."

"I'm not a child!" she protested angrily. "I'm almost twenty-one and...."

"From where I stand at the age of thirty-eight—eighteen years older than you, Emily—you are indeed a child," he replied gently. "Please believe me when I tell you that you are mistaken in your feelings for me. You must go back and resume your life in London. I promise you, my darling, you will find someone to love. Someone who will be nearer your own age and who will love and look after you. Believe me."

"I—I can't go back to that life—not now I've found you Ludo," she sobbed, unable to prevent the hot, frustrated and frightened tears from trickling down her face. "You don't...you don't understand...."

"Emily!" The cold, harsh tone of his voice hit her like a blow as he roughly shook her shoulders, swearing under his breath. She watched with dazed, tear-filled eyes as he got up and went to lean his head against a tall tree for a moment, before coming back to stand looking down at her. The moonlight threw his cheek-bones into sharp prominence, and she could see the deep lines of strain about the firm hard line of his mouth, the cold and stony glitter in his grey eyes.

"I have been trying to explain to you as kindly as I could, the true, hard facts of the situation. I now see," he ground out harshly, "that I must be brutally frank. Emily, I had a job to do and now it's over. I was instructed to rescue you and deliver you to a place of safety with all speed and despatch. This I have done. The fact that we found each other attractive and that I took advantage of your innocence, is an unfortunate side issue. As is, also, your mistaken belief that you have fallen in love with me."

He looked down at the woman sobbing bitterly on the bench. "Oh, darling Emily, can't you see that the time we spent together wasn't 'real'? It was—" he swept his hands distractedly through his hair "—it was an idyll—time out of mind. Surely you can see that it has little to do with the real life that you and I normally live. You must believe me when I tell you that you will look back on this short episode in your life, and be eternally grateful to me for having pointed out the harsh facts of life."

"How can you be so—so cruel?" she cried in agony, rising to face him on legs that were weak and trembling. "You know that—that you're condemning me to a miserably lonely and desolate life. A way of life that I hate and despise. I—I thought that you—you loved me," she moaned helplessly. "But you don't. You—you don't care for me at all!"

"*Damn it!*" he swore thickly, the words being torn from deep inside his chest. With a low groan he seized her by the shoulders, staring down at her tortured face in the moonlight. Almost blinded by her tears, she flinched at the blazing ferocity she glimpsed in his eyes.

A moment later he brought his expression under control.

"It's late and you have a long journey tomorrow," he said heavily, dropping his hands and turning away. "Good night Emily."

Stunned, she looked blankly at his tall, averted figure. She couldn't stop shaking as though held firmly and deeply in the grip of some tropical fever, her eyes as dark as sapphires and empty of everything but the agony which seemed to fill her whole existence.

"Was it—was it for this that you rescued me, Ludo?" she managed to whisper at last. "It—it would have been kinder of you to have left me to die...."

Her grief-stricken, tormented words hung in the still, humid night air, echoing about his rigid figure. "Oh Emily...!" he groaned huskily and turned, only to find that he was standing quite alone in the deserted, empty garden.

JULIE AND MARC looked at each other in consternation as Emily's slim, sobbing figure ran through the sitting room and listened to her footsteps echoing down the corridor until she reached the sanctuary of her bedroom.

After a while, Ludo walked slowly in from the garden and sat down in a chair, clasping his head in his hands. Some moments passed before he raised his strained face.

"I...er...I wonder if you could take Emily to the plane tomorrow, Marc? She seems to be a little upset and it might be best...."

"Oh, no!" Julie interrupted him in a hard voice he had never heard her use before. "Marc is going to be much too busy, here with me."

"Julie—I...." He looked at her with astonishment as she jumped up and left the room, banging the door behind her.

Ludo turned his questioning eyes to Marc. "Surely you can understand..." he pleaded, gesturing helplessly.

"No, I don't think we can," Marc said quietly as he left the room.

Ludo shakily lit a cigar and lay back in his chair, staring at the ceiling for a long time.

Julie knocked on Emily's door, and went in. The English woman lay across the bed sobbing as if her heart would break. Julie knew that there was nothing she could say or do that would help, but she sat down and put her arms about Emily and tried to comfort her.

After a while, Emily stopped crying and lay worn out, her head on the damp pillow. "I'm—I'm so sorry, Julie," she muttered. "I...I'm not being very grown-up, am I! It's just the thought of having to go back—back alone to the life I left...." She began to sob. "I don't know how I can bear it...the days and months and years of sterile life...all alone—without Ludo." She began to sob quietly again.

Julie got up and went to the bathroom, coming back with a cold flannel. "You do not have to go. You can stay here with us for a while if you like," she said, bathing Emily's red eyes with the cold compress.

"That—that's so kind of you," Emily hiccuped as she fought to control her sobs. "We haven't met before today and you've been so sweet to me." She found a handkerchief and blew her nose. "I can't accept, Julie, not just at the moment. Maybe later...oh!" she gasped. "I love him so much...I love him with all my heart...." And she began to cry again.

"I know," Julie murmured soothingly.

"He doesn't love me...he doesn't love me at all. He wouldn't...he couldn't do this to me...not if he cared!"

"*Ah, chérie*, I do not think it is as simple as all that. You see, I have known Ludo all my life. I was only a small girl when he rescued me from the burnt-out shell of my parents' house in Stanleyville." She smiled into the anguished blue eyes in front of her. "You must join a long queue, my dear. I and many others have been in love with Ludo all our lives! Not really, of course, but a sort of romantic dream—you understand!"

Emily nodded silently.

"His first marriage...." Julie shrugged. "He was only a boy, and she ran away after two months. He has always said that he was so shattered that he would never love again, but me—I am not so sure. Of course, since then he has had many, many women. He is a warm, passionate man, yes?"

Emily blew her nose in the vain hope that her handkerchief would hide the deep crimson tide she felt sweeping over her face.

"Now Emily," Julie said briskly. "It is maybe wrong of me to build up your hopes too much. However, I must tell you that Ludo is not behaving at all like his usual self—oh, no. He is the cool English gentleman—yes? His affairs have always been very light—very friendly. Always with mature women who 'know the score' as you say in English. But he is not behaving very well, is he? Oh, no, now he is very hard, very disagreeable, *n'est-ce pas*? So maybe he does care for you. It is possible."

She doesn't know that Ludo is furiously angry with himself at having taken my virginity, Emily thought in despair. It was only because he felt he had behaved badly, that he wasn't being "very light—very friendly." It was sweet of the French girl to try and cheer her up, but it was a hopeless task, almost as hopeless as her love for Ludo....

"Oh, hell..." Emily cursed weakly as she felt the miserable tears begin to trickle down her cheeks again.

"*Chérie*, to cry will achieve nothing. You must be strong and have courage. Surely you do not have to resume your old life, to become again a social butterfly, if you do not want to? You have a great deal of money.

Can you not use it profitably, rather than waste it on a life you hate? I do advise you to think about it. There are many unhappy people in this world, far unhappier than you can possibly be—even at this moment. Maybe you can do something for them and help yourself at the same time?"

"Yes. I—I will think about it, Julie, and—and thank you."

After the French girl had gone, Emily undressed slowly and crawled trembling between the cool sheets. She lay awake a long time as images of the time she had spent alone with Ludo chased themselves across her memory. She would never be the same person as the one he had first met. After having fallen so deeply in love with him, it was impossible for her to resume her empty life. A life without Ludo would be unbearable....

She fell asleep at last as the early light of dawn lit the sky.

Emily stayed in her room the next morning, until it was time to leave for the drive to the airport. She had refused any breakfast and Julie didn't push her to eat anything, merely bringing her a cup of hot, strong coffee.

Marc knocked on her door, calling out that it was time for her to go. She took a deep breath and walked out with her head held high, carrying her jewel case— the only luggage she possessed.

Her farewell to Julie was a tearful one, but she had herself under some sort of control as she walked out to the large Renault which Marc had lent to Ludo for the journey. Silently she climbed inside and waited for Ludo to join her.

He came out of the house. It was the first time she had seen him that day, and she was distressed to see how tired and strained he looked. Julie having lent her some dark glasses, she thankfully put them on before he got into the car beside her, and without a word started the engine.

The drive to Yaoundé took two hours, two hours of silence between them. Emily was in torture every minute of their journey, acutely and sensitively aware of every movement Ludo made beside her, aware of the dark hairs on his muscular arms and the musky scent of his aftershave. At last, as they arrived at the airport, her control gave way and she broke down into sobs she could not control.

"Oh, my darling, my sweet one." His arms went about her trembling figure as she leaned weeping against his shoulder.

The contact with his hard, firm body was more than she could bear. "Don't—don't send me away, Ludo... please!" she begged.

"I must, Emily—I have no choice. It will be best for you in the end, you'll see." He wiped her eyes with his large handkerchief, and slowly disengaging himself from her trembling figure, he got out of the car and came around to help her out.

Ludo led her over to the departure lounge, where he left her for a moment before returning with her ticket and an envelope. "You will have to change aeroplanes at Dovala for the flight to London, and this—" he gave her the envelope "—this contains enough money to see to your expenses during the trip plus your temporary visa. The British Consul has been very helpful..." his voice trailed away as he looked at her.

"Ludo..." she moaned in anguish as he clasped her in his arms, holding her tightly and burying his face in the fragrant curls of her hair. His body shook for a moment and then he relaxed his firm hold, stepping back and turning abruptly to stride swiftly away.

The tall, thin, white-faced woman watched his departing figure until it was out of sight. Her eyes blank with pain, Emily stumbled blindly towards the aeroplane that was to carry her far away from the man she loved.

CHAPTER NINE

EMILY HURRIED OUT of the presidential palace, glancing at her watch. She was behind schedule, she noticed with annoyance, as she quickened her steps towards the waiting limousine. Henry, her chauffeur, held the door open, smiling broadly.

"You're late, Miss Emily," he said as she slipped into the rear seat.

"I know," she agreed. "I hope poor Patrick isn't sweltering in this heat." She felt a pang of guilt as she thought of her pilot having to wait out on the runway. The midday sun of Ouanda in the hot season was unbearably fierce. "You'd better drive as fast as you can to the airport. Have you got my luggage?"

"Now, Miss Emily." Henry grinned at her in the mirror. "Would I forget? That housekeeper of yours, she's been like a cat on hot bricks—yes ma'am! She put the cases in herself: 'Just you make sure you don't bring Miss Emily back here,' she said to me. 'I don't want to see her for a full month,' were her final words!"

"Oh, Henry!" Emily laughed weakly, lying back against the leather seat. "It's all a conspiracy."

"Sure is!" he smiled as he drove swiftly through the crowded streets of the Ouandan capital, Dekoa.

Conspiracy was putting it a little strongly, she thought with a faint smile. Her doctor had been nagging her for months to take a holiday, and at last James Martin had put his foot down. "Either you take a break, or I'll give you my resignation," he had said firmly, and looking into his stern eyes she had bowed to the inevitable.

The question of where to go had been solved by Julie and Marc. They had suggested that she borrow the house of Julie's aunt on the shores of Lake Victoria in Kenya. Apparently the elderly lady was in Switzerland for her health, and the house was empty for the month of August.

"Here we are." Henry's voice cut into her thoughts, as he swung the car through the wide gates of the airport, slowing down so the man at the gate could recognise Emily. He promptly waved them through, and Henry drove across the tarmac to where her private Lear jet aeroplane was waiting.

Flying in and out of the country so often as she had this last year, did at least mean that she had very little hassle with the formalities, Emily thought gratefully as the limousine came to rest by the small jet.

"I'm sorry, Patrick, I got delayed," she called to her pilot as he leant against the wing of the aircraft. "Henry's just getting the cases out...." She paused, and put up a hand to shield her eyes in the bright sunlight. "You're not Patrick...!" she said with astonishment, looking around her in bewilderment.

"No, Miss Lambouchere. Patrick was taken ill last night and has asked me to substitute for him. He was apparently very anxious that you shouldn't miss your first holiday in a year."

Emily looked hard at the tall Englishman. After a year of speaking mostly French, the sound of an upper-class English accent sounded odd—especially on the sun-baked and windy runway of Ouanda airport.

"There is absolutely no problem. I have filed your flight plan, and the control tower are waiting for us to depart. If you'd just step inside, Miss Lambouchere, we can be off," he said firmly but pleasantly.

Emily looked at him doubtfully. He certainly didn't look like any pilot she had ever seen. Well over six feet, the dark uniform seemed to fit somewhat incongruously on his broad-shouldered, slim figure. His cap was tilted forward in what could only be called a rakish angle, over wavy dark hair that was far longer than the normal regulation length.

"Are—are you sure you're a pilot?" she asked perplexed. "I mean—you do know how to fly this machine?"

He smiled, the white teeth contrasting with his deep tan. "I don't believe in committing suicide this early in the day, Miss Lambouchere! Let's get airborne, shall we?"

She shrugged, turning to see that Henry had taken her cases on board while she had been talking to the new pilot. She said goodbye to her chauffeur and climbed aboard, going over to sit in one of the wide leather seats and doing up her belt.

"Everything all right?" The Englishman put his head around the door from the pilot's cabin. She nodded, and he disappeared.

Some time later, airborne at last, Emily went into the small galley and poured herself a glass of fresh orange juice, before coming back to sit down and look idly out of the window. James is right, she thought wearily, I do need a holiday. It's been a long year.... She lay back and closed her eyes, the rhythm of the jet engines soothing her tired brain. When she had boarded the aeroplane at Yaoundé airport in the Cameroon, a year ago, she would never have dreamed that she would or could have returned to Ouanda.

The journey back to London had been horrific. They had made an unscheduled stop at Algiers airport, and it was there that a local newspaperman had first picked up her name, flashing the news through to Reuters in London. When they had landed at Gatwick, she was amazed and terrified to find that she was being welcomed back as some sort of heroine. Emily had hurried through the crowd of waiting reporters, refusing to give any interviews, but nevertheless, she had woken up the next morning to find herself front-page news.

"Glamorous Socialite Survives Jungle Terror," was typical of some of the headlines in the Sunday papers. Arriving home on what journalists call a "slow-news day," her escape from the mercenaries had provided just the sort of story that appealed to the British public. There wasn't much hard copy, mainly pictures of her arrival looking drawn and tired, still in the clothes Julie had so kindly lent her.

Some papers contrasted that picture, with others taken some months previously when she had attended the Caledonian Ball at Grosvenor House, in Mayfair. Even Emily had managed to laugh wryly at the difference between the sophisticated, glamorous figure wearing a diamond tiara and necklace, a tartan sash draped across her sparkling white dress, and the thin, tall, unhappy and frankly rather scruffy-looking girl, trying to force her way through the crowds at Gatwick airport.

Emily had lain low, refusing to go out and stubbornly turning away all requests for an interview. However, her plight had caught the public imagination, and it was some time before an oil slick released from a sinking tanker drove her name from the newspapers. During that period there had been much speculation as to her mysterious rescuer, and one of the more scurrilous papers had published a story, *My Life with the Pygmy Headhunters* — a work of pure fiction.

Emily told her servants that no one—absolutely no one—was to be admitted, and she refused to accept any telephone calls. Thankfully, most of her old friends were away from London in August, and she spent the three weeks after her arrival in complete seclusion, going over and over in her mind during the long days and even longer lonely, torturous nights, the short time she had spent with Ludo.

There was no way that she was prepared to face life

on the old treadmill, as she regarded her previous existence. She realised that she must—somehow—lock her overwhelming love for Ludo away, deep in her heart. Never again, she promised herself, would she float idly by, like a swan on the river of life. She must, whatever the cost in terms of time and effort, endeavour to make something constructive of her life. The life she had so nearly lost. . . .

On Emily's twenty-first birthday, a day spent alone as usual, she received a letter from her trustees, congratulating her and requesting that she make an appointment to visit their premises in the city to talk about her future plans for the company. That night she sat out in the garden, making a list of all the things she thought she could do with her life.

It was a pitifully small list. All she had to contribute was a great deal of money, which together with energy and drive, seemed to be her only attributes.

She had finally come to a realisation and acceptance that Ludo could, and would, never return her love. But he had given her a precious gift—her life. Since he had never been prepared to accept any thanks for his action, the only way she knew of repaying him was to try to pass on to others less fortunate than herself, the gift that had been bestowed on her: to restore health; to provide clean living conditions; and to bring education to the illiterate. Surely that would be worthwhile? It would perhaps, in some strange way, prove to be an expression of her love for the man who had so changed her life.

First thing the next morning she rang an employment agency, and requested that a temporary secretary should be sent around immediately. She and the middle-aged woman liked each other from the first moment they met, and Miss Gilbert was now a permanent and valued member of her staff.

Miss Gilbert had immediately begun to carry out

Emily's instructions. Honouring Emily's promise in the rain forest, Pierre Lambouchere's diary of his epic voyage down the Congo River had been carefully wrapped and sent by special messager to Ludo's London flat, to await his arrival. Secondly, Miss Gilbert had rung Paris and ordered a collection of simple summer clothes, size ten, to be sent to Madame Julie Roget in the Cameroon. The directrice of Saint Laurent's Boutique collection had been very helpful, promising to expedite matters, Miss Gilbert reported; although, as she told Emily, it seemed a pity not to patronise an English couturier.

"No Frenchwoman worth her salt would agree with you!" Emily had retorted with a smile, and then passed on to other matters before leaving to meet her trustees.

At the end of a month Miss Gilbert and Emily felt they could look back with satisfaction at what had been achieved. Emily had attended a board meeting of her company, and had made it plain that she wanted certain changes to be made—fast. Many of the old guard who were not in sympathy with her plans were being pensioned off, while some bright young men had been "head-hunted" from other smaller city institutions, and would be joining the company soon.

Through the French government, she had instituted tentative negotiations with the new president of Ouanda. Her approach had been welcomed, and she had flown out to meet him. She had felt nervous and afraid as she flew into the country she had left so precipitately, but she and Edovard Dolle, the African president, had liked each other immediately, and he had agreed to all her plans with alacrity. He had promised to find the land for two orphanages to be built and staffed by her company, while she had guaranteed to rebuild the main hospital which had been damaged in the recent war. Plans were also made for her company to begin building a modern housing estate, with shops and a school.

Perhaps she was proudest of winkling James Martin away from his pygmies to run the hospital. She had helicoptered into his village, and it had taken her two days to persuade him that while the pygmy villagers would miss him, he had so much more to contribute to the new hospital, in the way of up-to-date medical care.

Dear James. She smiled to herself as she looked out of the aeroplane window at the clouds passing by. What a tower of strength he had proved to be. Something jogged in her mind and she looked around the cabin of the aircraft, a frown on her face. Something was wrong, and she couldn't place it for the moment. Everything looked very normal. The sound of the aeroplane engines gave her no cause for alarm, and yet.... She turned to look out of the window again, and then realised what was wrong. The sun! It—it wasn't in the right place. They were flying west and not east...!

She jumped up and went forward to the pilot's cabin. "Hello," said the pilot turning to look at her with a smile as she eased her way in and sat down on the seat beside him. "It's quite easy—do you want to take a hand at the controls?"

"No, I don't!" she snapped. "I want to know just what's going on? This plane seems to be flying in a westerly direction.... Where in the hell do you think you're going?"

"I know exactly where I'm going, Miss Lambouchere—there's no need to worry."

"Worry? Why should I be worried?" Emily regarded him with angry blue eyes. "Just what do you think you're doing, Mr. Whatever-your-name-is?"

"My name is Charles," the man said with a sideways grin, leaning forward to flip a switch and adjust one of the dials in front of him. "There, that's better." He eased off his headphones. "We're now on 'George,' the automatic pilot. Don't touch anything—there's a good girl—I'd hate us to end up smashed to pieces down there on the ground... very nasty!''

Emily said a rude word, regarding the man with fury. He had taken off his jacket and cap, and was wearing a short-sleeved white shirt which fitted tightly over his broad shoulders. He looked hard, tough and dangerous, and she tried to repress a nervous tremor as she began to realise that something was very wrong indeed.

"As to what I'm doing," he said, turning to face the angry girl. "I'm simply carrying out orders, that's all. There is absolutely nothing you can do. Why don't you go and sit down in the cabin? We've got about an hour to go; the time will pass very quickly, you'll see," he said soothingly.

"Don't you dare to patronise me, you...you flying bandit!" Emily shook with rage. "I demand to know where we're going!"

The strange man laughed. "I was warned that you might prove to be a bit of a handful! As to where we are going—there's no reason why you shouldn't know. It's Príncipe."

"Príncipe?" she echoed blankly. "But that's... surely that's a small island in the middle of the Gulf of Guinea, isn't it? Why are we going there? Is this a kidnapping? Because if it is, you're going to be out of luck. I've got no relatives who'd care a fig if I lived or died; so you're wasting your time."

"Yes," he answered with a maddening smile. "I suppose it is a sort of kidnap. However, money isn't involved. Why don't you go and relax in the cabin?"

Emily looked at him coldly and steadily for a moment, her mind racing. It must be political, she decided. If it really wasn't for ransom as he'd said. "I don't know what you're being paid for this little caper," she said slowly, "but whatever it is, I'll double it to turn this aeroplane around. That would seem to be a fair offer, don't you agree?" She forced herself to smile and held her breath, hoping that he would take the bait.

"As offers go—it's very good," he agreed with a grin. "However, I'm sorry to disappoint you, but I'm doing this for nothing. Just helping out a friend, that's all. Now, buzz off—there's a good girl—and leave me to fly this plane."

Struggling for control, Emily took a deep breath, looking longingly at a spanner fixed to the wall of the pilot's cabin. Dearly as she would like to brain him with it, there was no way she could possibly take over and fly the aeroplane. She was stuck and she knew it. "If that's the sort of friend you have," she hissed, "I'd hate to meet one of your enemies!" She left the seat and went back to the cabin, banging the door as hard as she could behind her, trying to ignore his sardonic laughter.

You're in a real fix this time, she told herself gloomily, as she threw herself into the wide, comfortable chair; and there's no Ludo around to rescue you. Ludo! Even after a year, the thought of him could still cause a shaft of pain to sear through her body. Most of her waking hours seemed to be spent in a frantic effort to make sure she was too busy to think about him. So busy, that by the time she found her bed every night, she was too tired to do more than lapse immediately into a deep sleep.

Three months ago James Martin had marched into her office and unceremoniously dragged her off to his consulting room. She had laughingly protested that she felt fine as he had silently given her a full physical examination, including X-rays.

"Sit down, Emily," he had said finally, "I want to talk to you, very seriously indeed. We both know that you are tough—but unless you make some alteration to your life-style, you will soon be in trouble. The blood test I took last week has led to today's examination. You are far too anemic. That can and will be remedied by some iron injections and a course of pills. But that's not the answer, is it?''

"Well, it's a start, don't you think?" Emily had tried to joke.

"Emily! This is me—James—talking. I'm your doctor—remember? This maniac rush to fill every hour so that you don't have to think of Ludo, is going to kill you sooner or later."

"James...I...that was all over a year ago...."

"Don't bother trying to lie to me, Emily. Not only am I your doctor, but I am also, I hope, your good friend. Ludo isn't worth it—believe me! Nobody's worth the price you are paying. This place isn't the hygienic United States of America, you know. It is very likely that in the near future you will pick up a bug I can't cure immediately, and which your undernourished and exhausted body won't be able to cope with. When that happens you will have to leave here—probably permanently."

"Oh, no! Surely not..." she protested anxiously.

"Oh, yes, almost certainly! I'm a damn good doctor and I know what I'm talking about. This place is plumb full of diseases that aren't even in the medical books yet, for heaven's sake! You must slow down and have adequate rest, or maybe you should see a psychiatrist. Something's got to be done."

"A...psychiatrist...? You must be out of your mind," she laughed nervously.

"Oh, no! It's your mind I'm worried about. I don't happen to believe that people die of broken hearts— and you're damn well not going to either. So make up your mind to have a long holiday—or I'll pack you off to London for good. And don't think I can't...I was at school with President Edovard Dolle, remember."

"I—I will try James, really I will. It's just that....."

"I know, Emily," he had sighed heavily. "If I could get my hands on that old friend of mine, that man you're so in love with, I'd wring his neck! In the meantime—you're going to have a holiday—right?"

"Yes, doctor," she had reluctantly agreed.

Now, looking out at the clouds, she managed a wry grin. So much for her holiday, she thought, wondering also if the alarm or a ransom note had already been delivered to her house in Dekoa.

Emily had soon found that if she wished to implement any of her schemes, she had to be on the spot, in Ouanda. So, leaving Miss Gilbert to hold the fort in London, she had transported herself to Ouanda nine months ago. She had found herself a house with a garden, and had installed a housekeeper since she still hadn't found time to learn to cook.

Despite her present predicament—who ever had heard of a kidnapper who didn't want money—she couldn't help smiling as she remembered her last weekend spent with Julie and Marc Roget. Julie had sent her a letter, thanking her for the dresses. "Now I'm the smartest woman in the Cameroon," she had written, and re-directed from London by Miss Gilbert, the letter had eventually found Emily in Ouanda. Emily had telephoned the Rogets and had gone to stay with them, being flown in the helicopter she had bought for James Martin. He mainly used it to bring seriously injured people to the hospital from outlying districts, and they had a scheme to try and run a flying doctor service in the future, when the hospital extensions were built.

That weekend in the Cameroon had been the first of many, and the Rogets had become her very good friends. Julie had tried to teach Emily the basics of cookery, but they had both agreed that Emily didn't seem to have a talent for it. It was during the last weekend she had spent with them, while she was ruefully regarding yet another cake that had sunk in the middle, that Julie had again broached the subject of Ludo.

Whenever James Martin or Marc and Julie had tried to talk about Ludo, Emily had adamantly refused to discuss the subject, or if pressed had simply left the room. Their relationship—the love she still had for him—had seared her very soul, and she knew that there would never be anyone else for her, this side of the grave.

"I know you don't want to talk about him, Emily," Julie had said, "but Ludo desperately wants to see you, Emily. He's been trying so hard for the past six months, but he says all his letters are returned unopened, and you apparently have such clout with the new president, that he has been sharply warned away from Ouanda."

"Not—not the rain forest and his gorillas—I'd—I'd never do that," Emily had said breathlessly.

"No, he knows that—but why won't you see him, Emily? It can't do any harm, surely?" Julie's eyes had been warm with sympathy. "I know what you went through, but it's been ten months now since you saw him. Surely you can forgive him?"

"You don't understand, Julie..." Emily said slowly. "I love him—I'll always love him—but I can't possibly go through it all again. I—I really can't. I still feel sick with longing for him. How do you think I could cope if I had to see him again?" Her eyes filled with tears as Julie put her arms about the tall woman, who was now so thin.

"You see? Look how silly I'm being...!" Emily blew her nose loudly. She thought for a moment. "You can give him a message, if you like, Julie. Tell him...tell him that he taught me to survive, and I'm—I'm trying to do just that, the only way I know how. He'll understand the message. Now," she had said with false brightness, "where is Phillipe? He's so busy learning to walk that he hasn't given me a cuddle for ages!"

Julie had looked sadly at Emily, and had not referred to the subject of Ludo again. Whether she had passed on the message, Emily never knew, because she had never asked.

Suddenly her ears began to pop, and she realised that the plane was losing height, which must mean that they would soon be landing. What was she to do, she thought frantically, looking around wildly for inspiration. All she had was her document case, which she had brought from the meeting with the president. If only she had a gun, she could drill him full of holes as soon as they landed. The blood-thirsty thought made her feel a little better, and she walked about the cabin, looking for something that would serve as a weapon.

"Fasten your seat-belt." The disembodied voice came through the loudspeaker as she returned from the galley looking more cheerful, and she settled down to face her forthcoming ordeal with as much resolution as she could manage.

The aeroplane came to a halt and the engines were switched off. In the sudden silence, Emily looked out of the window. On her side of the aeroplane there was nothing to see, except a sandy shore and blue sea. Undoing her belt, she went over to look out of the other side of the aeroplane. A black, mountainous range filled her vision, and she suddenly felt very frightened and alone.

The door was opened and the steps let down. "Come along, Miss Lambouchere. Your carriage awaits you." Charles, the kidnapper called out cheerfully. She went slowly over to the opening, the cool sea breeze whipping up her skirts as she looked down into his smiling face.

"I...I'm frightened," she said in a small voice, which would have raised the eyebrows of anyone who knew her. "You're—you're going to kill me. I—I know you are...." A tear, from the lemon juice she had just squeezed into her eye, trickled down her cheek.

"It's all right, don't worry," he said in a kinder voice, coming up the steps towards her. She stood, as if hesitating for a moment, and he stretched a hand forward to help her down the steps. She immediately lashed out at his body with her foot, and with her left hand, swung her hard case at his head. The unexpected force sent him reeling. She waved wildly at him with a kitchen knife from the galley as she flew down the steps, making for a grove of trees the other side of the small runway.

She never reached them. Half-way there, she heard his pounding footsteps, and was brought down by a flying rugger tackle. She lay dazed, bleeding from cuts to her knees and arms, as he picked her up and carried her lightly over to a waiting Jeep, parked beside some other light aircraft on the runway.

"Tsk, tsk," he clicked his tongue and grinned, while placing her in the passenger seat. "What a very naughty and wicked girl you are! I'm lucky that you missed your aim with the knife. I was warned, but you looked so angelic with that mop of blond curls...come along," he added, putting her case in the back and getting into the driving seat. "There's someone who wants to see you—and good luck to him!" he laughed grimly as he started the engine.

Emily could barely suppress the tears of anger and mortification as she sat in the bumpy Jeep, dabbing her grazes with a handkerchief provided by the hateful Charles. They seemed to be following the sea-shore, and she closed her eyes as her head began to ache and throb from her fall.

After some ten minutes they arrived at a long, low house set on the beach. If Emily hadn't been so dazed, sore and angry she would have appreciated the trailing vines and flowering shrubs which surrounded the green lawn. They came to a stop by the front door, and she briefly said a prayer as she turned to regard her abductor with stony eyes.

"You can walk or I can carry you," he said cheerfully. "Which?"

"I'll walk—you...you rat!" she hissed through clenched teeth, stiffly climbing out of the vehicle and limping slowly in front of him towards the door.

"Rats are sadly misunderstood creatures," he said blandly, ushering her into a cool bedroom with blue-and-white curtains billowing at the windows. "This is your room and that's the bathroom through there. Please don't try and escape. It's much too hot to have to chase you and there's really nowhere to go. Okay?" He gave her a wide grin and left, locking the door behind him.

Sometime later, having bathed her cuts and grazes, she was sitting disconsolately on a double bed, when she heard a vehicle draw up. She limped to the window, but could see nothing and went over to put her ear to the door. At first there was an indistinct buzz of conversation, followed by a loud laugh as footsteps approached. Her eyes grew wide and she stiffened in shock as a rich, dark voice laughed again, and said, "You can't say I didn't warn you Charles—it serves you right!"

Emily staggered back as the door was opened and, at last, she stood face to face with her abductor. "Ludo...!" she gasped. Everything began to whirl about her eyes, and the floor came up to meet her as she collapsed in a dead faint.

CHAPTER TEN

SLOWLY SURFACING from a dark mist, Emily opened her eyes to find herself lying on the comfortable cushions of a large sofa in the main room. Ludo was bathing her forehead with a cold flannel and looking down at her with tender eyes, full of concern.

"It—it really is you, Ludo...?" she whispered, wincing as she raised a trembling hand to feel a bump on her head.

"She's a holy terror—a proper little hell-cat, Ludo, and all that I can say is that I wish you the very best of luck!" Emily's hateful kidnapper stood by the door, smiling at them both as he juggled a bunch of keys.

"You—you bloody man...!" Emily gasped, struggling to sit up. "I should have killed you with that spanner in the cabin, when I had the chance! Only—only I didn't know how to fly an aeroplane," she moaned tearfully. "Just you wait, Mr. Charles What's your-name...I'll—I'll get a gun and...."

"Oh, my darling Emily—you haven't changed a bit!" Ludo laughed softly as he gently pressed her back on to the cushions.

"See what I mean, Ludo! I'm off now—give me a yell if you need any help, old boy. I must warn you that my money's on Emily—what a girl!" Charles left the house, roaring with laughter.

"Who—who's that dreadful man?" she asked, closing her eyes as her head began to throb and ache.

"He's my cousin. His wife owns a large part of this

island. You'll like him when you get to know him, Emily."

"You must be mad! I—I have no desire to further his acquaintance and...if you don't give me something for this headache," she groaned, "I'll—I'll die...."

"You poor darling," he said, coming back with a glass. "I've dissolved two aspirins in some water; they should begin to work soon." He sat down beside her, helping her to sit up and drink the liquid.

"That was foul, ugh!" she grimaced, her face beginning to colour as she felt his firm, strong arms about her.

"What are you doing here?" She looked at him in bewilderment, suddenly remembering all the extraordinary events of the day. "And—and what's more to the point, what am I doing here?"

"This is my house and you are here for a holiday. It took a bit of fixing, but it seemed the only way I could manage to see you, Emily." He smiled down into her eyes, her face only inches from his own as he held her tightly in his arms.

"I—I didn't want to see you, ever again," she whispered, shutting her eyes. The feel of his warm embrace was so comforting that for a moment she relaxed and imagined it could always be this way. But she knew it couldn't and she struggled to break free.

"I—I must go...I can't stay here..." she murmured huskily. "Please let me go, Ludo."

"I'm sorry, Emily. It's just not possible. Here you are and here you'll stay. The holiday will do you good. James tells me that you are desperately in need of some rest, and I agree with him. Darling girl, you're looking far too thin and not at all well. It's time you rested and let other people worry about the poor and underprivileged of this world for a while."

"*James?*" she gasped. "He knows about this—this

kidnapping?'' She looked at him in astonishment, her dazed mind in a whirl.

Ludo nodded and gave an unhappy laugh. "He took some persuading. Several long telephone calls, in fact. But I convinced him that I had your best interests at heart and he eventually agreed to co-operate—as did Marc and Julie."

He laid her gently back on the sofa, wringing out a flannel in cold water before folding it and putting it on her forehead. "I don't know what you've done to all my friends, my love," he smiled tenderly down at her. "It has seemed for a long time as though I was Public Enemy Number One!"

"Oh, Ludo...." Emily looked at him in distress. "I never meant... I mean... I don't understand. I—I don't think I can cope with all this...." She blinked and turned her head away from his warm, grey eyes, looking blindly out of the large picture window as she felt a tear slide down her cheek.

As it began to slip down over the horizon, the setting sun had turned the sea to red; and she shut her eyes tightly before any more tears could escape and betray her unhappiness.

"Darling Emily, it's been a long day. I'm going to give you some hot soup and pop you into bed. We can talk about everything tomorrow. Now just lie there and I'll be back in a moment with a tray."

He returned to find that she had fallen into an exhausted sleep. Ludo stood for a long time looking down at her, his mouth tightening grimly as he saw how thin and worn out she looked. He walked out to the Jeep and removed her cases, taking them into her room before coming back and carrying Emily through to her bedroom, placing her gently on the bed. He proceeded to swiftly undress the woman, and roll her between the sheets, bending down to give her cheek a soft kiss.

Emily murmured his name, opening her eyes briefly to smile at him before falling asleep again.

She woke up the next morning, her limbs still aching from the bruises and cuts she had sustained while running away from Charles. Thankfully her head no longer seemed to be throbbing, although her fingers could feel the outline of a small lump on her forehead. With a deep sigh, Emily lay back on the pillows and tried to come to terms with the almost incredible fact that she was, to all intents and purposes, a prisoner in Ludo's house.

There seemed no possibility of escape. How on earth, she wondered desperately, could she be expected to cope with his constant proximity? How could she bear to see him day after day for a whole month, and then have to part yet again? She moaned softly in distress as she felt her stomach contract with the old, familiar ache of longing for his warm embrace.

It's so—so cruel of him, she thought with resentment. She'd managed to make some sort of life for herself. Lord knows it wasn't much—but an existence of sorts, nevertheless. Now he'd... well, he'd forced his way into her life again, deliberately disrupting her plans and shattering the defensive screen she had so laboriously built around herself. Why, oh why couldn't he have left her alone?

She sat up, stiffly easing herself off the bed and moving slowly over to look out of the window. The long sandy beach and the clear blue sea looked so inviting that she felt a sudden longing for a cool swim. Going over to her case she opened it and removed one of the new bikinis she had bought for her holiday. From the corner of her eye she caught a shimmer of movement in the long, full-length mirror and turned to look at herself more closely.

Her face blanched with horror as she suddenly realised that she was naked. Ludo must have undressed

her when he put her to bed last night! A tide of deep
crimson washed over her white cheeks as she quickly
slipped into the thin scraps of material.

She'd never been as thin as this, she thought with
dismay, looking at her slim body, inadequately covered
by the skimpy, pale blue bikini. In fact the only part of
her anatomy that hadn't slimmed down was her bust,
which only seemed to look larger in contrast to the rest
of her slender figure. Heaven knows what Ludo will
think, she groaned to herself, and then blushed again
as she realised that it should no longer matter what he
thought. But it did, of course, she sighed, turning miserably away from the mirror to grab a towel. Relieved
to find that her door wasn't locked, she moved silently
through the empty house and out on to the deserted
beach.

Emily tried to ignore the sharp sting of the salty sea
water against her cuts and grazes, relishing instead the
feel of the cool waves on her heated body. She swam
about for some time before turning over to float lazily,
enjoying the feel of the early-morning sun beating
down on her skin.

"You look better already." Ludo's deep, rich voice
came from behind her. Startled, she floundered in the
water for a moment before she surfaced, spluttering
with confusion.

"My, you gave me a fright!" she gasped, treading
water as she realised that she had floated out beyond
her depth.

"My darling girl. I can't possibly let an investment,
on which I have spent two months of my life, float out
to sea, can I!" His warm laugh and the glint in his eyes
made her blush with confusion. She hurriedly turned
away and swam for the shore.

"Come on, we're going to cook breakfast," he
called, passing her in the water with a smooth, lithe
crawl. She watched as he reached the sand and climbed

out of the water. Breathlessly she looked at his deeply tanned figure as he stood waiting for her to join him, and despite the morning sun she shivered, her heart pounding in her breast as she slowly waded towards him. There was a disturbing gleam in his grey eyes as held out a towel, draping it gently about her shoulders before leading her to a pile of brushwood, besides which lay some wet fish on a large green leaf.

"I went fishing early this morning. Come and sit down, it won't take long for them to cook—I am about to prepare you a feast for the gods!"

"I'm surprised you didn't ask me to gather the wood," she said without thinking, and then blushed scarlet as all the suppressed memories of their journey together came back vividly into her mind.

Ludo cast her a swift, searching glance, before silently turning back to cook their breakfast. Looking at his broad, tanned back, Emily strove to compose herself, her mind in a daze. This man had caused her more pain than she had ever known in her life. She ought to feel a burning resentment of the way Ludo had treated her, both in sending her back to London and in arranging the "kidnapping" yesterday. But strangely, she didn't.

Gazing at his lithe, bronzed figure, she realised with a sudden feeling of weakness that he was all she ever wanted from life. She despised herself for being so spineless, for the overwhelming feeling of happiness and joy at being in his company once more. She didn't know how she was going to manage to get through the next month of her holiday, but she knew she would treasure every moment of every day, to hold warmly in her heart against the cold years ahead.

But why? Why had he brought her here to this island? Surely he couldn't really be as cruel as his actions seemed to prove? He had deliberately rejected her love and need for him a year ago. Why should he now suddenly decide to see her again, and have gone to such dramatic lengths to do so?

The thoughts ran through her head in a confused stream, tiny flickers of almost unbearable hope alternating with long stretches of depression as she silently ate the meal prepared by Ludo.

"That was...er...delicious," she said, licking her fingers. In truth, she hadn't tasted the fish at all, being totally preoccupied and absorbed by her involved speculations as to exactly why Ludo had brought her to this island.

"Not only am I a brilliant cook, I had the forethought to make up a thermos of coffee," he said blandly, handing her a cup. She sipped the hot, steaming liquid, her hands shaking nervously as she stared blindly out over the blue sea, aware that Ludo had turned his dark head and was regarding her intently.

The silence lengthened between them. "It's—it's lovely here," she said at last in a small voice. "Have you...have you lived here for long?"

"Only for about eight or nine months," he replied. "After...well, after our journey, I had to go to Chicago to advise the zoo on their gorilla house and then I came back to London. I—I looked for you everywhere, Emily." His voice was quiet and low as he stared out to sea. Emily's heart began to thud loudly, and she found she was having considerable difficulty in breathing normally.

"First of all, I had a hell of a dust-up with some old dragon at your house in Knightsbridge. After I'd managed to get past that butler of yours—and that took some doing, I can tell you!"

"Miss Gilbert," she murmured. "She never said anything to me about it...."

"Well, she said plenty to me! She seemed to regard me as the devil incarnate for some reason." He gave an unhappy bark of laughter. "She refused to take back your great-great-grandfather's diary and also refused point blank to give me your address. I—I felt like a small, scrubby schoolboy by the time she had finished giving me the rough end of her tongue."

"Oh, Ludo, I . . . ."

"Nobody knew where you were—or so they said. Your trustees, I may add, were singularly—and I suspect deliberately—unhelpful as well. It speaks volumes for your character and personality, my darling girl, that you should be able to inspire such loyalty, although I can't say I appreciated it very much at the time."

Emily flushed and gazed down blindly at her coffee. There seemed to be a large constriction in her throat, and she somehow wasn't able to stop the trembling in her hands.

He threw a log on to the fire. "I even tried some contacts of mine on one of the London papers. The word was that you had disappeared. Nobody had a clue where you'd gone. Julie and Marc Roget weren't talking to me—I nearly went out of my mind!"

"I . . ." Emily tried to clear her throat. "I—I'm sorry, Ludo," she murmured hesitantly. "It really . . . it really wasn't a deliberate policy . . . not at first. I—I was so busy and . . . well, after I went to live in Ouanda . . . ." Her voice died away.

"My first clue to your whereabouts came when I decided to find solace with the gorillas." Ludo turned to smile wryly at her. "Sounds a bit mad, doesn't it? I called to see James and found he had disappeared. It seemed that 'a white, golden-haired goddess had arrived from the sky in a flying machine and had transported him to Heaven.' Well, that's how the pygmy chief put it, and a check with the medical register in London told me where he was. After that, I managed to make a few phone calls and put two and two together."

"Ludo, I'm . . . er . . . I'm sorry you had such a—a search." Emily's heart was pounding fiercely and she suddenly felt quite sick. "But—but I don't...I mean, why were you looking for me? I—I don't understand," she added breathlessly. "You said we must never... ever meet again...."

There was a long silence as he gazed intently at her averted face. Sighing heavily, he turned to stare out to sea. "I've—I've been such a bloody fool, Emily," he said at last, his voice thick and husky with emotion. "It...well, it nearly broke my heart to send you away. God knows I—I thought I was doing the right thing, my love—" He broke off to pass his hands distractedly through his black hair.

"You were so pure—such an innocent. How you ever managed to stay like that mixing with your dreadful crowd, I'll never know. But you were so very young and I—I took away your innocence..." he groaned.

"Oh Ludo..." she breathed. "It wasn't important...."

"Yes, yes it was my darling." He sighed deeply, still sitting with his back to her looking blindly into space. "During our journey I—I came to see that I was practically the only person who had ever cared deeply for you. How could I let you throw yourself away on the first man to show you any love, any kindness? Oh, my dearest, darling Emily, I loved you far too much to do that."

Emily's jaw dropped and she turned to gaze at him in open-mouthed stupefaction, totally unable to believe what she was hearing.

"I was certain that the right and proper thing—if I really cared for you—was to send you back to London. I...well, I almost broke down at the damn airport. I was nearly sick with worry about what would happen to you; how I stopped myself from telling you how much I loved you and begging you to stay with me...well, I'll—I'll never know. The moment your plane took off, I knew it was all a ghastly mistake, and I've been in

torment ever since. Oh my dearest, dearest love...
please, oh, please forgive me!''

He turned, deep lines of strain etching his face as he
put out his hands beseechingly towards her. Without a
moment's hesitation, as if it seemed the most natural
thing in the world, Emily gathered his unhappy figure
into her trembling arms, cradling his head against her
breast. Murmuring quietly, she rocked him lovingly in
her embrace.

"My dearest—how I love you!" The raw hunger in
his voice was reflected in his grey eyes as he sat up and
cupped her flushed cheeks with hands that shook with
emotion. Breathing as if the effort pained him, he muttered huskily, "I'm never going to let you go again, not
as long as I live. Oh, *Emily* ...."

He groaned deeply, lowering his dark head and finding her mouth with his own, possessing it with a blind
urgency that swept aside all barriers between them.
Emily clung to him, trembling violently with a need
she could no longer even attempt to deny, murmuring
soft, incoherent cries of delight as his mouth moved
from her lips to cover her face with soft, gentle kisses.

"Oh my sweet, sweet Emily. I was so worried that I
might lose you. It's been such a long year and I feared
that you might—might fall in love with someone else.
You're so young and ...."

She placed trembling fingers against his mouth, smiling at him in a daze as she struggled to comprehend
what he was saying. "Do you really mean ...? Are you
really saying that—that you love me?"

"Oh, my dearest love!" he laughed shakily. "It took
me weeks to convince James of that. I hope to heaven
it won't take me as long with you!"

"I—I can't believe it...." Emily began to cry helplessly, totally overwhelmed by waves of sheer happiness.

"Don't cry, my sweet. Please...." He held her

tightly in his arms kissing away the tears that flowed down her cheeks.

"It's just...." She smiled tremulously at him through eyelashes still wet with tears. "It's just that I can't...I really can't believe it's possible to feel so happy...." She put up a hand to touch his cheek in wonder and joy as he smiled tenderly down at her.

"I hope to spend the rest of my life convincing you, every day, how much I love you," he said thickly, gazing down into her lovely face. "Starting right now, this minute..." he whispered softly, brushing her lips delicately with his mouth. The soft gentleness of his kiss brought tears of joy to her eyes, and she felt his powerful body shake as he once again, after so long, tasted the full sweetness of her mouth.

"My darling," he murmured, slowly and reluctantly removing his lips from hers to cover her face with soft, fleeting kisses. "I... er...I had it all planned. A quiet dinner, a long speech...the lot! But... I...oh, Emily, my lovely, beautiful Emily, I—I can't wait. Please say that you'll marry me. I can't live without you, my darling. I really can't...." His arms tightened convulsively about her slim form as he anxiously awaited her answer.

Emily looked up into the handsome face of the man who meant so much to her, remembering his first wife and his forthright views on the idle rich. Because she loved him with all her heart and because, quite simply, his happiness was more important than her own, she made herself ask the last and most important question. "Money, diamonds and all...?" she whispered, closing her eyes and praying to all the gods as she had never prayed before.

"Money, diamonds and all...all my love as long as I live," he solemnly vowed.

"Oh, Ludo!" She buried her head in his shoulder. "I feel quite weak with happiness. I...oh, yes, please. I mean...yes, I do want to marry you. I...."

"You're not the only one who feels weak with happiness, my love!" Ludo trembled with relief as he held her tightly in his arms. "What a wonderful girl you are!" He kissed her gently, looking down into her radiant blue eyes shining mistily at him, reflecting back the tenderness and love in his own.

They lay quietly together as the sun rose in the sky. Presently, Ludo suggested that they have a swim to cool off and then return to the house for some more coffee.

"I'm still worried about my age, darling," he said, holding her hand as they walked down to the sea. "Eighteen years..." he sighed. "It's a big gap between us."

"You poor old man!" Emily grinned. "Never mind, grandpa. We'll get you fitted out for your wheelchair next week! Ow!" she squealed as he proceeded to pick her up and throw her into the water.

"Em-i-ly!" he growled with twinkling eyes, diving in beside her. "You are, without doubt, the most incorrigible girl I've ever met. A wheelchair!"

"I can remember," she said dreamily, her jaw aching with the effort to keep a straight face. "I can remember the night I first met you. I told you then that I didn't think you looked a day more than fifty-five!" She burst out laughing and shrieked as he grabbed her slim figure.

"I tell you what," she said, breathless from his firm, determined kiss. "I think the whole question of your age is a raving bore—almost as boring as my money. Let's forget about them both, shall we?"

"Agreed," he said promptly as his hands began to sensually caress her body.

"What...er...what about coffee?" she murmured, suddenly feeling nervous and apprehensive. Not for any good reason of course, she told herself, as Ludo gazed so lovingly down into her eyes. It was just that it had been over a year since...well, since they'd made love. He might be disappointed now that she was so thin and.... For a year she hadn't bothered to care what she looked like.... Maybe Ludo would regret asking her to marry him?

"Come along, my shy bride," he said, interrupting her confused and embarrassed thoughts. He took her hand and led her from the sea up towards the house. Emily glanced quickly at him through her eyelashes, blushing as she realised that he had clearly read her mind. "Go and put on a dry bikini," he said as they entered the building, "while I get us some coffee."

"Yes, *Herr Commandant*!" She grinned and escaped into her bedroom. "What I can't understand," she said on her return a few minutes later, "is what you are doing here on this island? And is that man Charles really your cousin? It all seems very strange to me."

"In fact, it's very simple," he answered, coming over to sit beside her on the big, wide sofa. "I was determined to find you and marry you, however long it took me. Since you seemed to be living permanently in Africa, I decided to base myself out here." He bent forward to pour their coffee.

"So, Dr. Ludovic Vandenberg resigned from London University, sold his flat, and was looking for somewhere to live when his cousin Charles suggested that he join him on this island. Simple really, my darling."

"Oh, Ludo! You can't have given up your post at London University for me? How awful!" Emily looked at him in distress.

"Do you know—I do believe that there's even less material in that bikini than the one you were wearing earlier, Emily! The more I see of you..." he burst out laughing as she blushed a deep crimson, dropping a light kiss on her shoulder. "You goose! I'd never do anything that I didn't want to. You should know that by now."

"What's Charles doing here? He's a horrid man—just like you!"

"He was in the Fleet Air Arm, hence his ability to fly. When I got your...er...message from Julie, two months ago, I knew there was nothing for it. I would have to kidnap you and keep you with me until you agreed to marry me! It took a bit of fixing, but with Charles' help I managed it. In case you are worrying about your pilot—don't. He is on an all-expenses-paid holiday on safari in Kenya at the moment, although he did say that if you weren't married by the time he returned, I would have to look out!" Emily gave a gurgle of laughter at his doleful expression.

"Don't you laugh at me, you witch!" he grinned. "There I was, none of my friends talking to me, except to tell me how foolish and stupid I had been. I've never felt so low and unhappy in my life! Oh, darling, I've been such a crass fool...if it hadn't been for Charles, I don't know what I would have done. His wife is a super girl and I know that you'll like her very much. Her father died and left her his cocoa plantation out here. The present government seem content to let her continue to farm it, so Charles sold up and they came to settle out here."

"I should have guessed he must be a relative of yours; he was every bit as horrid to me as you were, when we first met...." She was prevented from saying any more as he slipped an arm around her slim waist, and leaning across her, brought his mouth down on hers in a satisfyingly long kiss.

"You know very well that I was deeply attracted to you, right from the start, you baggage! I thought I'd never seen such a lovely girl—that come-hither look you sent me across the terrace at the Sinclairs' party made my toes curl!"

"Things...well, things deteriorated rather quickly after that," she said sadly, remembering the dreadful row between them that night and the beginning of their journey.

"Oh, don't remind me..." he groaned. "Looking back—and I've had a whole year to think things over, my love—I think I must have fallen for you like a ton of bricks, straight away. I...er...I really don't make a habit of going up to a girl and kissing her before I even know her name, you know! When Bob told me who you were...darling, I can't explain my actions except to say that it felt as if I'd been knifed in the stomach. I'd been footloose and fancy-free for over sixteen years. Never in all that time had I fallen in love with anyone. Can you understand how I felt when I discovered that a girl, whom I already instinctively knew was going to be desperately important to me, came from the same ghastly world as my first wife? I really can't remember what I said; there seemed to be a sort of red mist in front of my eyes. I don't think I've ever been so angry and frustrated in my whole life!"

"Oh, Ludo...I thought you were insane, I really did!" Emily laughed weakly.

"Darling, I think I must have been temporarily out of my mind. You're right, I was simply foul to you. For most of the journey too," he added gloomily. "I—I got myself into such a mess. I didn't approve of your background, as you know, and yet—and yet there I was, falling more madly in love with you every day."

"Well, I was a nasty spoiled brat, wasn't I!" Emily leaned against his shoulder. "You soon sorted me out..." she said, beginning to shake with laughter. "Do you remember that first supper in the bush? 'Eat up or I'll ram it down your throat!' you said, and I believed you—you certainly would have...!"

"Please, Emily!" He shrugged helplessly. "I was so worried that you wouldn't stay strong and fit; it's so easy to become ill in those sorts of conditions. Not," he grinned, "that I needed to worry. You were absolutely splendid. I became so very proud of you, so full of admiration for your courage and tenacity. What a wonderful girl you were—and are! Anyway, I soon realised that you were not superficially brittle, that it was just a pose, a protective cloak to prevent yourself from being hurt and rejected. It became almost more than I could bear to keep my hands off you, and of course I gave way to temptation.'' He sighed heavily.

"Thank heaven you did," Emily told him dreamily. "I wanted you to make love to me so much that I nearly died of frustration!"

"Don't talk to me about frustration! The night you lay in my arms in the rain forest, after your nightmare...! I can still remember it now. All I could think about, all night long, was how we'd made love by the waterfall. You were so pure, so innocent and inexperienced, and yet within your arms I had experienced something I have never known with any other woman— a wonderful, mystical blending of mind and body.'' His voice became thick and hoarse as his hands slipped erotically over her warm skin, his mouth once more possessing her soft, welcoming lips.

"Oh, Emily," he whispered shakily a few moments later. "I must get Charles to rustle up a clergyman to marry us as soon as possible!"

"Oh, yes..." she breathed ecstatically, and then struggled to sit up as her eyes clouded with concern. "Ludo, what are we going to do in the future? I mean...what about all the work I've been doing in Ouanda? I'd forgotten all about it for a moment."

"Dearest girl—you must do what you think right. I don't want you to drive yourself as hard as you have been, that's all. I've got a new assignment to do a long TV series on the gorillas in Guinea and I want you there with me, of course. Can't James take over and run the set-up instead? If you went there a few times a year, just to see how things were going.... I don't want to be selfish, but I need you every bit as much as the starving orphans."

"Darling Ludo—that's a marvellous idea! Most of the groundwork is done now in any case. I can tell him to get anyone he needs to help him, and he'll run it perfectly. The diamond company virtually runs itself, and you can sort out any problems that might arise."

"Hang on! It's not my scene, Emily," he said, suddenly looking stern.

"How can you say that?" she looked at him mournfully. "It's cruel of you not to look after your children's inheritance. They won't thank you, you know."

"My what...?"

"Honestly, Ludo," she grinned. "We are going to have babies, aren't we? Lots of little Vandenbergs running around? I think about six would be nice."

He laughed. "How about four to start with, my darling Emily? Yes, of course, I hope we'll have children—if they all look like you it will be perfect." His arm tightened about her waist.

"That's settled then," Emily said firmly. "Since I really do intend to be a wife and mother first and foremost, you can't possibly expect me to breast-feed a baby at company meetings, can you? You will obviously have to take over, won't you? I never gave a snap of my fingers for the money or the diamonds. As far as I'm concerned you can run the whole thing and I will settle down to being a domestic wife. How lovely," she sighed with contentment.

"Well, my love, I think I'd better do the cooking," he said with a loving grin, as his hands began to slowly stroke her body. "I hear from Julie, who says she will forgive me if I marry you with all speed and despatch, that you still have a long way to go in the kitchen!"

"That's not fair," she said breathlessly, the touch of his warm fingers causing tremors of delight to dance over her skin. "I—I'm much better than I was...."

"Nonsense—I've heard all about the cakes that sink in the middle!" he teased, as he gently and slowly removed her bikini top, exposing her warm, creamy breasts, the tips swollen with desire. "So beautiful..." he murmured, his voice dark and thick with passion as he trailed his lips over her body.

"Julie...Julie says my omelettes are...are very good," she gasped as he swept her up in his arms, carrying her swiftly into the bedroom.

"My dearest love," he said thickly as he lay beside her, his touch becoming more pressing, more intimate. "If I'd wanted you as a cook, I'd have said so. As it is, do you think that you can concentrate—just for the moment—on fulfilling the role I have in mind for you?"

Emily gazed up into his handsome, smiling face, at his grey eyes gleaming with passionate desire. Forgetting all her fears and shyness, she wound her arms about his neck, burying her fingers in his hair.

"Now that," she said, with a husky gurgle of laughter, "that presents no problem at all!"